Blackwater

Abe Dancer

A Black Horse Western
ROBERT HALE

© Abe Dancer 2016
First published in Great Britain 2016

ISBN 978-0-7198-1856-1

The Crowood Press
The Stable Block
Crowood Lane
Ramsbury
Marlborough
Wiltshire SN8 2HR

www.crowood.com

Robert Hale is an imprint
of The Crowood Press

Printed and bound in Great Britain by
CPI Antony Rowe, Chippenham and Eastbourne

Blackwater

Jack Rogan decides to return home from years of gambling on the Mississippi riverboats, but he makes a big mistake when taking what he thinks is a shorter, faster route back to Texas.

The Louisiana swamplands are teeming with all sorts of dangers, not least Gaston Savoy and Homer Lamb, and their kin from the secluded waterside community of Whistler.

Captured and stripped of his money, his guns and his fine sorrel mare, Jack is compromised into making a deal with his captors.

Meanwhile, a faction of corrupt businessmen decides to make a move on the valuable timber that spreads throughout bayou country. When they hire professional gunmen, Jack discovers the main reason for his capture; and learns just what is expected of him.

1

Jack Rogan had just finished a late breakfast in the Blackwater hash house. Sitting in the pungent interior, he was on his second cup of coffee, listening to low voices from a table somewhere close behind him. He was trying not to get interested in the way of their conversation when his attention turned to the opening of the screen door. At first there didn't appear to be anyone entering, but then he looked down and saw the dog.

It was an elderly coon hound, and it came in limping, had dark wheals across its shoulders from which the blood had flowed and clotted. It hobbled with one forepaw held away from the floorboards, a bewildered look of fear in its lustrous eyes.

'Jeeesus, feller, who the hell you been mixing with?' Jack said, easing himself from his chair. He dropped to one knee to stroke the animal's head, but no sooner had he moved, than the screen door slammed full open. A gaunt young man with long white hair, stomped in, didn't bother looking up.

The dog immediately cringed. It whimpered and tried to slope away, attempted to avoid the stout switch that snapped down at him.

With a curse, and a wince from aching bones, Jack got to his feet. Using big strong fingers he grabbed the man by the wrist with one hand, whacked him very solidly across the side of the face with the other. Then he let go, watched steely-eyed as the tormentor staggered back out through the rusted screen.

Losing balance, the man dropped his whip and fell from the sidewalk into the street.

Jack followed. With a meaty shoulder, he shoved open the screen door, ripping it away from its top hinge. He stepped out, lifted the toe of his boot and kicked the whip away from the boards, set himself to consider the situation.

The fallen man was Blanco Bilis. He lived in a fishing shack, bankside to the Village River, usually came to town in the evenings when he'd sit on the boardwalk opposite the High Chair Saloon, watching the dancing girls descend the steps from their rooms above. Now, dribbling wet dirt, he ran the back of his hand across his mouth. Lying on his side, he stared around in wild temper for whoever it was who had hit him.

'Touch that old dog again, and I'll take that stick to your bare ass,' Jack threatened.

'What the hell's it to you?' Bilis scoffed.

'Nothing much. But it might be to him.'

'Stupid, interferin' pokenose,' Bilis snarled, furious and humiliated. He pushed his right hand into his jacket front, drew the short-barrelled pistol from under his left arm.

Jack, not seeing a gun around the man's waist was waiting for such a move, was already in the street. He took two steps towards Bilis, lashed out hard at the man's gun hand. He shifted his considerable weight and ground his foot down until Bilis gasped and released the gun into the acrid dirt.

'Little hideout gun, you gutless son-of-a-bitch,' Jack rasped, then stamped on the fleshy part of Bilis's nose. 'Now you've been slapped, kicked and squashed. Unless you want worse, I suggest you get right back to wherever you belong,' he added.

Bilis made a protective move towards the front of his face, cursing thickly, almost choking on the drama.

'You'll be seeking vengeance at your peril, feller. I'm past being too young to indulge in second chances,' Jack warned as he turned away.

The hound limped out onto the sidewalk. It lowered its head, took a short look at Bilis, then a more thoughtful one at Jack.

Jack returned the look. 'I'm not long in this town so I can't look after you,' he said. 'Pack your traps and find some new quarters. That hobble should sucker most folk.'

On the trail away from Blackwater, Jack was going to head west. He'd decided to bend south, make his way through bayou country, away from the Mississippi Delta, cross the Sabine River into Texas. The land was swathed by lakes and ponds, cut by creeks and bayous. But it was good thinking time, and he was in no hurry.

In ten years, Jack had accumulated more than $1,000, mostly from playing stud poker on the paddle steamers that plied between Baton Rouge and New Orleans. Now, he wore a store-bought suit, carried a new .36 Navy Colt and rode a fine sorrel horse. The ride to Beaumont was going to be his last real journey, make the circle just about a full one.

Travelling through the unknown country was his choice, but it made him jittery. When he'd proposed taking the short cut into Texas by heading south around the big lakes, he'd been vividly advised against it.

'Swampers,' the Blackwater liveryman had said, spitting in the dust as if something offensive had come to mind. 'Land's just crawlin' with 'em. They live so close to the water, some say they come from *under* it.

It's a fact, they drink turpentine an' eat snake. They get 'emselves lathered up over nothin' an' think with their goddamn squirrel guns. You wanna go *above* the swamps, a *long* ways above, not through 'em. Take that as a friendly warnin', feller. They ain't nice people,' he stressed, just missing Jack's feet with another line of chaw tobacco juice.

'Yeah, I think I might have already met one of 'em,' Jack replied, already deciding not to heed the advice. 'If and when you hear of trouble, head straight for it. By the time you get there, it'll most likely be cleared up,' his pa had once told him.

But now the moon was fading fast and the cypresses were closing in on him. Thin layers of mist rose from the still backwaters, and bullfrogs and crickets were laying down their carpet of night sound. Jack was thinking it wasn't the most comforting country he'd ever ridden through, that his pa's words weren't the most appropriate.

He shivered, grinned confidently as he turned and put the sorrel into a slow run of creek water. 'At least I'll be laying me a soft bed tonight,' he called, waving an arm at the thick Spanish moss that festooned the surrounding cypress trees. He started to look out for a good campsite, something with good all round cover, somewhere he'd feel safe sleeping.

Shouldn't be too difficult, he thought as he reined in.

He held the sorrel very still, turned his fingers around the butt of the Colt at his hip. 'What was that?' he mumbled, his eyes peering into the murkiness. A big, blue heron launched itself from a tangle of submerged roots, flew directly overhead with heavy wing beats. He took his hand off his gun and watched the prick of his sorrel's ears. 'It's a bird,' he offered, gently heeling forward. 'We've spent too long in civilization.'

Jack didn't know much about the clandestine ways of the people who inhabited the bayous, but he'd been told not to ignore them or take them for granted. So he'd take precautions: make his camp well back from anything that appeared to be a track; have his horse stand off from the bedground. And he wasn't going to light a fire. Maybe he'd even set up a trip ring before climbing into his blanket.

Jack was three hours into what was, for him, an uncommon open-air slumber. It was a shallow sleep, and he was mostly awake when the song of the night critters suddenly ceased.

He didn't see the shadow that moved in the yellowy, moonlit glade. He was telling himself not to make a move, to keep very still, even though instinct wanted him to react. Whoever was approaching would likely have a gun trained on him, would probably pull the trigger at his slightest waking movement. *Wait until I know he's more fully occupied. Like when he's touching me,* Jack thought and suppressed a shudder, prepared himself for the moment.

Having grown to adulthood in the wilderness, hunting everything from alligators to snapping turtles, Cletus Savoy could usually walk the bayous without disturbing a sleepy catfish. As if mimicking the heron, he now stood completely still beside a drooping cypress. He carried a sawed-off scattergun; had one pale-blue eye on Jack, another on the trees that screened the sorrel.

The man lowered his head, licked his lips hopefully. The Savoy clan had always been prowlers and opportunists, had indulged in most sorts of thievery. Only thievery wasn't how they saw it. To them it was a means to an end, a way of existing, and Cletus had to exist like any other living soul in and on the water. And right now, Cletus was thinking it had been a long time since he'd any cash funds, an age since he'd poured freely from anything other than a crock of moonshine.

But, for many months, Uncle Gaston Savoy had been trying to progress the family's reputation. On a long trip to New Orleans, he brushed with civic improvement, acknowledged the error of 'old ways'. He had also realized that new law enforcement did indeed have long and resourceful arms.

As a close relative, one of the first victims of Uncle

Gaston's attempt to convert had been Cletus. There was no crossing Uncle Gaston, and until this night, many light-fingered deeds had been curbed. But Cletus prided himself on having a sharp eye for anything in its prime, and the moment he caught wind of Jack Rogan's sorrel he knew there was something to be had, regardless of family obligation.

He didn't know Jack was carrying a large amount of money, but every wily instinct told him there was something else to be had along with the horse. The words, 'Hide nothing from your minister,' came to Savoy. It was something his uncle was fond of saying, and Savoy thought it somehow fitted the situation.

He took a few steps forward and hunkered down, let the fingers so used to noodling catfish, go about their illusory work.

Jack gritted his teeth, tried to keep a steady rhythm with his breathing. He stilled himself, resolved only to make a move when whoever was robbing him moved off. Shoot the unknown sneak thief in the middle of his back.

The feeling of holding the crammed billfold caused Cletus Savoy's pulse to pick up a beat. He eased away soundlessly from Jack's unmoving form, but his heart was racing with expectation. He just knew he'd suddenly got rich, and in a few more minutes, he'd be that and well mounted to boot. Maybe the richest and best mounted man in the county. And what would Uncle Gaston have to say about that, he wondered.

As Savoy approached the sorrel, he moved like smoke, curling and drifting through the dark, tupelo boles. But, like Jack Rogan, the horse's heaviest slumber was never that deep, never that insensible. Its ears pricked, one eye opened and it let out a sharp, night-cracking whinny.

This is the moment, Jack thought. He exploded from his sugan, his Navy Colt sweeping up in one smooth motion.

Cletus Savoy turned one way then the other. Momentarily, he stood transfixed under the waxy moonlight, his jaw hanging open.

'You're not stealing from me, you son-of-a-bitch,' Jack rasped.

The swamper took off with a lame-legged scuttle, and Jack fired. He was a fair shot with a handgun, but Cletus Savoy's run was unpredictable, gave little to shoot at.

Cletus Savoy made it back to the trees where he'd stashed his mule. Clutching the billfold and the scattergun, he managed to swing himself up and into the saddle. 'Run for the hollow ... fast,' he shouted, thinking he'd make it away.

Cletus Savoy knew the surrounding country like the back of his hand, that the man chasing him, was a total stranger. What he didn't know was, the horse Jack was riding was a clear-foot and faster than it looked. With a large moon beaming down across the watery land, there were only a few safe boltholes. Savoy had to run, but for every ten strides his mule covered, the sorrel was gaining.

The riders covered a long mile at a wary pace. They rode around a bayou that opened into a broad lake edged with hundreds of ancient root coils and gnarled stumps. It was on the far, western side of the dark water, where the land started to clear, that Jack quickly started to close in.

As Cletus Savoy galloped his mule through the narrows, he fired two barrels of bird-shot into the sky. It seemed the frantic reaction of a man gripped by panic. But if Jack had eased up to think about it for a moment, he might have guessed it was some kind of a signal.

A mile further on, Cletus Savoy rode towards a clearing of glistening eel grass. The moonlight and shadows cast against the backdrop of cypress and oak created a site of dark foreboding.

Ahead of him, Jack saw his quarry slow, dragging back on the reins. He guessed the man was either going to surrender or make a stand. With his Colt held out before him, he ran the sorrel into the glade. 'Just make a stand,' he rasped, stating his preference.

Savoy's weary mule stood splay-legged, its head drooping, sweat coursing down the insides of its legs. The rider sat his saddle with hands raised to shoulder height. There was an odd, unconcerned expression on his face that Jack didn't figure out, thought it might be that the mule wasn't going any further.

'Goddamn you,' Jack panted, but threatening and gritty. 'Make one more move and I'll put a couple more holes in your runt face.'

Cletus Savoy was careful not to blink. He didn't raise his hands any higher, not even when the clearing came alive with a chorus of threatening, mechanical clicking noises.

Jack understood what was happening then. But before he could do anything, he was surrounded by half a dozen actioned firearms. Each was gripped in the hands of a smirking swamper – men whose faces appeared to be identical to that of the man who'd robbed him.

'Looks like rest o' litter turn up,' Cletus Savoy said, with an unnerving, low-pitched snigger.

2

A cool breeze worked its way between the trees and the heavy swags of mossy foliage. It brushed the surface of the water, moved the misty carpet into bankside rolls. Ragged clouds scudded across the face of the moon, brought a lower level of darkness to the lake.

A raw-boned hand relieved Jack of his Colt, while another seized his arm and hauled him to the ground.

Jack shook the man's hand away, gulped air as a gun barrel pushed viciously against his chest. He'd been involved in more than a few fights and confrontations before, but never under circumstances like this. With their moonlit faces and pale eyes staring back at him, Jack's adversaries showed signs of real malevolent purpose. He knew his predicament rated as one of the most scary he'd ever been in.

'So,' said a beanpole, whose voice already sounded like it was going to enjoy the question. 'What we got us here, Cletus?'

Cletus Savoy was breathing easier. He'd not ridden home, but to Frog Hollow, a customary muster point for friends and family when one of them was in trouble. He'd been thinking that, if he hadn't made it, this man in the store-bought suit might well have run him down, already turned him into alligator meat. His legs still held a tremble, but no one could see. He reached out and pinched Jack's cheek. 'A real, pink-flesh trespasser is what we got,' he replied.

The other men were slightly tentative, but they moved in on Jack, as though he was up for sacrifice. They remained silent, moved their rifles around under their arms. They were lean, fair and pale-eyed, big-eared like Cletus Savoy. But one of them was a redhead, another had broader shoulders, wore a long straggly beard. Their common feature was the cold, unkindly stamp on each of their faces.

'Ain't that so, pink man?' Cletus Savoy continued, poking his finger into Jack's midriff.

'Up close, you really are one ugly son-of-a-bitch,' Jack said quietly. 'And you're making a big mistake doing that.'

Cletus Savoy's face slowly crumpled into a sneer as he took a half step back. It brought him within range of Jack's boot, which crashed up into his groin. He jack-knifed, spewing as he hit ground.

Someone swung a rifle butt and Jack grunted, fell

heavily alongside Cletus Savoy. His head rang like a range cook's iron as he took a foot in the ribs. His fast assessment of the situation was that one man among a group was less likely to kill in cold blood, than if he was on his own. *So, let's check this out*, he thought wool-ly-headedly, as he spat and cursed, forcing himself back onto his feet.

One of the group immediately shoved a gun up under his chin, breathed fetid breath into his face. 'What you chase Cousin Cletus for? You after him or his mule? Would've done both, eh, if we hadn't been about? Now you gone an' likely squash his bean.' The man rubbed the ball of his thumb across the hammer of his rifle. 'Hell, we slit an' spit men for less 'an that … feed the hogs, even. You best think on a prayer, mister, 'cause you sure goin' to die.'

But Jack sensed, hoped, this was some sort of voodoo talk. Blinking all emotion from his face he stared ahead, saying nothing.

The men glowered at him expectantly, waiting for him to break down. They looked thwarted when he didn't, possibly slowed by their confusion.

Powerful hands hauled an ashy-faced Cletus Savoy to his feet, pushed and propped him against a black stump knuckle.

'All right, let's hear it, Cletus,' said the long-bearded man. 'What's your story?'

'I'll save you some time,' Jack started in. 'You'll find my billfold somewhere about him. Go take a look. But who … *what* are you to believe. That I wanted *his* crow bait mule, or that he wanted *my* sorrel?'

Cletus Savoy gave a slow confused shrug. 'Hell, Homer, you say we's to make our own way when we can. That's what I was doin'.'

'Let me see the billfold,' the man called Homer said.

'Heck it's mine, Homer. I took risks.'

'Give me the man's goddamn poke,' Homer grated. Snatching the billfold from Cletus Savoy's belt, he pulled it open.

'Hell an' Judas,' the redhead, Loop Ducet snorted ahead of all the others. 'Must be a million dollars there.'

'Not quite,' Jack said. He knew down to the last cent how much money he had, and meant to get it back one way or another. He still carried his pocket revolver – his private indemnity – tucked into his trousers in the small of his back. The swampers hadn't discovered it yet, but that didn't surprise him. It was fundamental stuff; they thought that what they saw was what there was. But through his gambling know-how, Jack was considerate of the odds. He knew that even with a pair of fully loaded, matched twin Colts in his fists and a carbine for backup, starting a fight against these sorts of odds would be extremely hazardous and foolhardy. These might be simple folk, but that didn't mean they were soft in any way, less than cunning.

Homer Lamb fingered through Jack's personal billfold, withdrew an addressed envelope. He read the words with care and raised a single eyebrow. 'John Rogan. Blackwater. Is that you?'

'Yeah. Blackwater's a place I used to be. The last place.'

'Hey, reckon I heard o' them *Rowguns*,' Loop Ducet, said, smoothing his hair and giving Jack an exaggerated, low curtsy. 'So, look up brotherly trash. We're in high class company. These *Rowguns*, they any kin to them *Rowguns* what come to pin us with accusations on whatever takes their fallutin' fancy? Are you them kind, Mr *Rowgun*?' he asked, stepping closer to Jack. He raised his face confrontationally, gave the full breathy effect of molasses and chaw tobacco.

'If I thought there was even half a brain inside that skull o' yours, I might dignify that dumb question,' Jack seethed. His fingers and knuckles itched and he balled his fists. He wanted to bust the man's nose, do something bad to his face. He'd done similar stuff before, in the confines of the paddle steamers when forcefulness was crucial. 'I just want to keep what's mine, same as you do,' he said, calmly. 'If you return my money with an apology, I'll be on my way. If not, I'll be obliged to find me a star-toter … make him a statement.'

'Yeah, I can see how you would be, you bein' a proper citizen an' all,' Homer Lamb broke in. 'But it's quite a ways from here to the nearest law, an' there's many a danger in between. Ain't that so, boys?'

Jack sensed that Lamb might be the leader of the pack. The man sniffed, spat and rolled his shoulders. He had an old Walker .44 tucked into a broad belt; a sheath knife hung from a loop of shoulder cord.

Heads nodded, made eager, petulant voices sounded. To Jack, the men looked like turkey vultures, eager to rip into their prey, but mindful of an inbred pecking order.

'Just hand me back my money and I'll be on my way. Nothing lost, nothing gained,' he said through clenched teeth.

'He'd offer us up anyway, I reckon, Homer,' Loop Ducet drawled, tugging at a bandolier of yellow rope.

'Maybe. Trouble is, messin' with the law's somethin' we ain't supposed to be doin' right now,' Lamb said broodingly. He turned to the sorrel, and his taut features appeared to relax. 'But this here young lady's an unforeseen event … makes things different,' he added.

He reached out to offer a cupped hand to the sorrel's nose, but the big head snapped down and teeth flashed. The man shouted an oath, drew back his chomped fingers and swung a retaliatory punch with his right fist.

The sorrel reared away and Jack leaped forward. His fist hammered straight into the meat of Lamb's mouth. The man went down, crumpling like a sack of sugar beet.

Jack reached for his pocket revolver as he wheeled away. But the others, who'd been waiting edgily, were on him, grunting with eager prospect. Jack knew that if he fell, it was odds on he mightn't get up again. Fearful of the worst, he quickly decided to go down fighting.

He felt the collapse of a smashed nose, the pain of his fingers cracking against a bony forehead. He saw two of his assailants fall, almost had time for a satisfied grin before a rifle butt hit him in the nape of his neck and the moon gave up on its big, waxy brightness.

3

The secluded community of Whistler was less than a mile from Frog Hollow. During daylight hours, most of its people kept to themselves. Night-time was usually more lively, with the men gambling, arguing and brawling amongst themselves. They swilled most stuff found in a jar, and smoked or chewed just about anything that was dead or close to it.

Melba Savoy was an early riser, usually one of the first outside, winter or summer. Slender, raven-haired and just eighteen, it was Melba's custom to roll from her bed around five o'clock. She preferred that part of the day, the peaceful time before sunrise. In a place so often made untidy by men, children, hogs and dogs, the early mornings were always something to look forward to.

Melba rose and dressed, washed her face and brushed her hair, paused by the faded Jesus likeness that was pinned to the wall beside the front door.

She said a few prayer words, thought it might help her family along the straight and narrow path so recently prescribed by Pappa Gaston.

She was ready to start her day, walking out onto the narrow raised deck that fronted the cabin. She listened to Homer Lamb's red rooster, as it warmed to its task of heralding another day, watched the wood ducks lapping up their weed around the fishing platforms. But a frown stirred her face when she saw the saddle mule appear from the back of the woodshed and head towards her vegetable patch. The animal belonged to Cousin Cletus, and obviously hadn't been tended to overnight.

Careless, or what, Melba thought. *Maybe he was too drunk to tend anything last night.* But she knew that the menfolk of Whistler always took care of their work animals before themselves. No matter what. Even Cletus.

Stepping off the deck, Melba went after the mule, caught it by the trailing reins and led it back to the woodshed. There was still no sign of anyone else, and she mused about some of them having an unusually late night. She'd heard them in the early hours, wondered where they might have galloped off to. 'Perhaps it was the Sabine Cuff,' she muttered. 'Perhaps they flushed it.'

The Sabine Cuff was a huge mutated bear of

legendary cunning and longevity which had, for many years, succeeded in making the best hunters in the county appear green. A great accolade awaited anyone who wound up sinking their bare toes in the beast's dark hide.

After giving the mule a drink, Melba walked across a compound that had been created within a dozen or more functional, but crudely built cabins. Wedged in between the forage store and the meathouse, smoke curled lazily from the chimney of the cookshack, a hang-around place for the bachelors of the close-knit community.

Women of a certain age were scarce throughout the wetlands, and certainly within the confines of Whistler. And girls in town tended to shy off whenever an unmarried man showed up with an eager grin, looking for some cosying. But Melba wasn't particularly worried or wary of them because they were mostly family. Of those who weren't, there were one or two she quite liked, but not enough for anything further. Now and again, someone would make a concerted effort, but she had a knack of discouraging the advance. Bumping egos was something you didn't do to impulsive, young male swampers. That she would look more kindly on a proposal from the Sabine Cuff might be what she felt, but it wouldn't be worth the saying, the upshot.

Homer Lamb refused to be one of the discouraged.

Unfortunately, of all the keen young men she knew, he actually would come second to the big, black bear. Smiling at the mixed thoughts, Melba continued on her way across the yard to the forage store.

On the side of the small building, in a narrow plot away from the wind, Melba had planted several squash. Her brother, John, had given her a sack of fertilizer made from dried grass and mule muck, had even dug it into the soil for her. The squash were growing fast, but required almost daily weeding in the rich loam. Melba drew a long forked stick from the soil, pushed the tip back in and twisted against the invasive shoots of mallow and foxtail.

'Weeds is weeds. No matter how much you fight 'em, they just keep on coming.'

The voice was so close and unexpected it startled Melba, making her gasp. She looked round sharply but saw nobody. A moment later she turned towards the nailed slats of the store's window hole.

From six feet away, a total stranger with a rugged face, a steel-grey moustache and eyes of almost the same colour, was peering at her through a gap in the crude wooden lathes.

'What are you doing in there?' she demanded, taking a step back.

'If it was some sort of field hospital, I'd say recuperating,' Jack Rogan answered. 'Perhaps those who put me here can tell you,' he added.

Her composure returning, Melba jabbed the forked stick back into the soil, squinted at him with open curiosity. The forage store had always been the spot where troublemakers were held, trespassers and snoopers, sometimes a violently drunk relation ready to do mischief to themselves as well as others. But there hadn't been anyone locked away for some time, and from what Melba could see, this prisoner was hardly a young tearaway, didn't fit into any of the accustomed categories.

A moment later, the penny dropped. A bunch of men riding off in the middle of the night had woken Melba up.... 'Let me guess. It was *you* my kin were after last night. Who are you?' she asked, thinking that the Sabine Cuff wasn't the cause of the commotion, after all.

'There's some folk call me Mr Rogan. That seems rather out of place at the moment, so just call me, Jack. Do you want to keep the advantage?'

'I'm Melba Savoy,' Melba said. 'Why are you locked in there?'

Jack frowned thoughtfully. 'I don't know. I really don't. It started off with someone robbing me. I was fast asleep and minding my own business.'

'You sound like a towner to me, and that could be reason enough. Those boys sure got an aversion to *them*.'

'Well I don't know about being a towner, as you put it. But I am moderately civilized,' Jack replied. 'Which is more than can be said for the gutless half-wit kin of yours. 'Specially the one who tried to break my neck.'

'If that had've happened, they would have fed you to the hogs.'

'Well, in this place here, it was hard to know I hadn't been. Took me a while to realize hogs move around a bit more than onions and goddamn goober peas.'

'Very funny. You must have done something quite bad for them to lock you away for the night. It was the same men, wasn't it?'

'Yeah, your kinfolk. I counted six of them. They probably took it in turns to whack me when I was out cold.'

'We're not all like that, Mr Rogan. You say they robbed you?'

'One in particular. I haven't worked out exactly who and what you people might be, or what the hell this place is, but an idea's growing.'

'Hmm. The one who robbed you. Have you got a name?'

'More like a breed. It was Cletus.'

'Cousin Cletus. I guess that makes some sort of sense. He's not the sharpest knife we've got.'

'Yeah. From what I've seen, he really hasn't got much going for him,' Jack said.

'Look, Miss Melba Savoy, I want out of here, so you go and shake awake whoever's at the top of your pecking order and bring 'em here.'

'You want to crack on with whatever punishment they've got in mind?'

'Not particularly. But if they were going to kill me they'd have done it already. The way it is, they're building up a big piece of trouble and you'll be included for aiding and abetting. Tell him that. I think his name's Homer.'

'That'll be Homer Lamb, but he's not the elder.'

'Bring anybody. If it can open up this goddamn shack, you can bring your dog.'

Beyond Melba, Jack saw a few men approaching and he didn't bother to continue. The man in the centre with the long, wispy beard and badly swollen mouth was Homer Lamb.

'He's not going to be too sympathetic,' Jack muttered to himself.

One man pulled away the bracing board and opened the door; two others dragged Jack out roughly.

'Homer,' Melba said, trying to intervene. 'What the deuce do you think you're doing? Has he killed someone?'

Homer Lamb dug powerful fingers into the top of Jack's arm, gave the girl a curt nod. 'Mornin', Miss Melba. Your pa wants to take a look at him.' Lamb gave

Jack an inhospitable stare. 'I guess he wants to take a look at the stranger who thought he could take us all on. Wants to know what he was doin' here.'

'What I'm doin' here is a strategy of yours, not mine. I was hoping to pass through, but one of you robbed me of my money while I was asleep. I was just exercising my right to get it back,' Jack answered. 'And where's my sorrel?' he snapped.

Lamb had his own thoughts on what was going to happen next. 'We'll see what ol' Gaston has to say,' he replied. 'But just in case somethin' needs to be stretched, Loop, get it prepared.'

The redhead, Loop Ducet, nodded. He didn't say anything, just grinned malevolently as he fingered his coil of rope.

For the shortest moment, Jack considered the possibility of escape. But he saw the language of their faces and knew they were ahead of him. It was what they wanted; an opportunity to call out the dogs. The decision not to break away was so reassuring, it almost took his mind off the searing pain across his shoulders, in his neck and head.

Lamb nodded and strong hands reached out, shoved him in the direction of the largest of the settlement's buildings.

Jack turned his head to glance back at Melba. Now he was hit low in his back, close to his kidneys. His knees went shaky, nearly brought him down.

'Straight ahead. Miss Melba ain't for payin' you any mind.' The voice then became a throaty laugh; Jack thought it was Cletus Savoy.

A puncheon door, mounted on fat leather hinges, swung out. A man, who practically filled the frame top to bottom, as well as from side to side, stepped onto a double-planked levee. He glanced at the still water before swinging his black eyes to Jack.

Jack cursed. 'Some of 'em come stacked high. He must be six-six,' he muttered, an obvious and shared thought of those watching and listening.

'Is this him?' the huge man barked. 'Him who's dis-turbin' the peace of our community … *my* community?'

Not for the first time, Jack got it into his head that he might have trouble getting out alive if he didn't come up with a probable story.

'Who are you, an' what you got to say for yourself?' the man continued.

'I'm Jack Rogan, and I'm riding west to Beaumont, Texas. I thought starting off south would be a good idea … save me a hundred miles or more. It was a mistake, but not one I should make an apology for.' Jack was hoping his frankness was akin to truth, the way to go.

'So why were you settin' about my boys?'

'One of them crept up on me in the middle of the

night and stole my billfold. It certainly weren't neigh-bourly. He was doing more of a trespass than I was. Haven't you heard of the Constitution out here? We've got one, you know. It's my right to take back what's mine.'

4

Gaston Savoy was the community patriarch, the one who had made Whistler their home, brought them in on the old float roads. For almost a decade, families had confronted hardship and prejudice, but they were tenacious and maintained a niche for themselves. What they couldn't steal or poach, they paid for in cash from selling eels and squirrel meat to the nearest towns west and north of the nearby lakes.

The head man of the community never had much of an inclination for tolerance. One hard look told him that Jack Rogan was the kind of outsider he felt most antipathy towards. Every accoutrement and gewgaw that the stranger owned would have been shop bought. With a fat billfold of cash money, there was nothing in common. Savoy decided to give Jack a rough time because of it, make a show with his men looking on.

'That's as maybe. Where'd you come from? he demanded. 'What sort o' line you in?'

'I played the boats on Big Muddy. That money's my grubstake, and Beaumont's my home. I was hoping to introduce the two.' Jack stared back. When it came to giving someone a cold, undaunted eye, he was up there with the best of them.

'A cardsharp, huh,' Savoy grunted as though another assumption had just been affirmed. Again he looked Jack up and down with gimlet eyes. 'Let me figure. You was figurin' on easy pickin's among the simple folk. Put on some lard.'

Jack was going to say how absurd the idea was, when Savoy looked towards the group of men. 'He tried to steal your mount, too, I hear?' he asked of Cletus.

You got to be some sort of idiot to believe that, Jack thought, and nearly smiled at the continuing foolishness.

'Yessir,' Cletus Savoy lied without hesitation, hawked and spat for emphasis. 'Then he tried to shoot me like a pot pig, Uncle. Can Loop hang him now? Can we run him?'

Although Jack sensed this was chiefly to scare him, he knew it was possible they meant the threats, to get the 'prey' warmed up. From what he'd heard, most swampers didn't acknowledge laws other than their own. It was how they had been schooled, how they managed to live their lives. But recently, Gaston Savoy had been looking hard about him, was thinking twice about this backward way of life.

'I've got folk in Beaumont who are expecting me back,' Jack responded. 'To be honest, they're looking forward to my money. So if I don't turn up with it, they'll come looking. And they'll hire more law than you ever thought existed. Half the Texas Rangers, most likely. So you wouldn't want anything happening to me, if you get my meaning.'

'Hmm. You mean your money's more important than your hide. Usin' that to frighten me, are you?' Savoy sneered.

'The cruster hit me when I weren't lookin',' Homer Lamb alleged, rubbing the back of his hand across his mouth.

'An' he was makin' cow eyes at Miss Melba,' another man weighed in.

They just want me dead and they're stringing it out … filling their time, Jack was thinking disappointedly. *Got to do something.*

'Why, the more I get to know you, mister, the more I'm inclined to let Loop have his fun. Is there anythin' you *ain't* done?' Savoy wanted to know.

'Yeah, *one* thing, you oversized lame brain,' Jack rasped, wrenching free of restraining clutches. He caught Savoy with a punch that swung hard and fast to the low side of the massive man's jaw. The patriarch of Whistler went a half-step sideways, then backwards before dropping to his knees on the raised walkway.

'Always wanted to go down with a winning hand. Guess I will be,' Jack said as pain exploded from his fingers to his wrist and forearm. He leaped forward, dragged a foot across Savoy's body and stumbled into the man's cabin. It was a big, single gloomy room, with pungent, feral aromas. Jack swallowed hard. In a brief, desperate moment, he had seen the cabin as an obstacle between the pursuers and a getaway path. And so far he'd got it right. The men didn't want to enter Gaston Savoy's dwelling, and with the sounds of cursing welling up behind him, Jack ran for a narrow, single door set in the far wall. Shoulder first, he cracked the door apart, saw it led nowhere other than a small platform at the water's edge. He cursed at the rank water and turned back.

'That's a real private place, pumpkin. 'You just come to me,' said a gravel-voiced man, wrapping arms around him as thick and hairy as a grizzly.

Jack thought it best if he went quietly. He let the tension go from his hands and arms, allowed himself be pitched back outside.

Gaston Savoy didn't bother to look up. He'd raised himself into a hunch, had closed his eyes, the tip of his tongue probing one side of his mouth.

The bemused, albeit cruel smirk on Homer Lamb's face did little to reassure Jack of his imminent future.

But he wasn't going to regret what he'd done; there seemed little alternative.

Savoy stumbled to standing. 'I suppose you're goin' to tell me that breakin' the jaw of Gaston Savoy was in the goddamn Constitution, too?' he rumbled.

Jack was about to say he thought it might be, when Melba stepped in between them, edging up close to Savoy.

Savoy made to brush her aside but she was persistent, stood on tiptoe, whispering behind her hand.

'I don't know about that,' Savoy grumbled, holding a great maw around the bottom of his face. 'But it might be savin' me the price of one o' them pricey jaw crackers.'

Melba kept on in a low voice, while the assembled men waited impatiently. Homer Lamb looked doubtful of the exchange, and Jack just stood there with his arms pinned back, his eyes opening and closing with ominous fatigue.

'I'm still goin' to flay him. The varmint tried to steal—' Savoy started, but Melba cut him short.

'Just stop it, Pa. You know very well that he didn't steal anything. Cletus robbed *him*, and everyone here knows it. Why, that money's bursting his pants apart right now. Forget how much you dislike outsiders and start acting sensibly. Someone with an eye to the future, you said, remember? As is the gander, and all that.'

'I remember, okay. Are you goin' to say he never laid a finger on our boys? He never done that?' Savoy continued.

'Take a look at him, Pa. A good look,' Melba invited. 'I mightn't know much about gambling and suchlike, but I reckon I've picked up something about men. What I see here is someone who could probably shoot holes in any of our fine family, take anything he wanted ... *if* he wanted.' Melba gestured around her. 'Do you see anyone carrying more holes than they should be, Pa. Do you?'

Savoy massaged his face, pushed two heavy fingers around a lower tooth. It was true he had a lot on his mind, didn't want to be wasting time, giving lie to his declared thoughts and wishes. But it was a long time since he'd taken a punch like the one from Jack. Likewise, since he'd taken his rawhide bullwhip to a troublemaker. And now his daughter was suggesting he consider other important matters.

'Of course you don't,' Melba continued, grimacing at the men. 'There's nothing to see other than a handful of blank heads. They're all lying, Pa, telling you just what they reckon you want to hear ... hitting you in the vulnerable spot. For goodness' sake, it was *them* who caused the trouble, and they're terrified of getting punished for it.'

'You know what happened, do you, Melba?' Savoy

asked as though losing a bit of interest.

'Yes I do, and I wasn't even there,' Melba responded quickly. 'Our Cletus jumped the man then got chased for it. He rode off, fired two warning shots, and the boys surrounded them at Frog Hollow. It's the procedure for trouble, Pa.'

Savoy was nearly there, just needed a few more moments to get his judgment sorted.

'This was meant to happen – him sort of dropping by. Take advantage, like any opportunist would. Are you going to be led by old creeds? *If you don't like it, kill it*, is out of date. You told us so. You're the one who wants us to have those civic improvements. It don't just mean doors and windows. We got to start learning about things, Pa. Got to.'

Nobody knew what Melba was talking about, except presumably, Savoy. Not Homer Lamb or even his sons, Eliot and John. All it meant to Jack was that his immediate future was being discussed, and it depended on Melba's line of reasoning – whether it worked on Savoy himself.

Jack turned his attention to Melba. It might not hurt to play up to her a little. She was speaking up for him – in a way. He attempted a look that wasn't far off a smile, something that expressed his thanks.

Melba reacted with a long cold stare.

It was immediately obvious that whatever the girl

was talking about, it was for her father and not for Jack. Nevertheless, it obviously didn't include him being flayed alive or strung from the nearest cypress.

Shortly, Savoy stopped his ruminations. 'Perhaps you're right … for some of it,' he accepted. 'Unhand him, boys,' he gestured. 'There's another way for me an' Mr Rogan to straighten things out. You can't smack somebody when your arm's around a crock o' shine.'

I'll settle for that, Jack thought, agreeable to the mystifying offer.

5

Sweat dribbled from the crumpled lines of Winge Tedder's brow as he watched Harry Grice push the blade of his skinning knife against the old treadle whetstone.

'It was those gunshots gave me the jitters. It was middle o' the night, sounded as though it was over Whistler way. I figured someone was coming to deal with me.' Tedder kept talking just to fill out the menacing silence. He ran the palm of his hand across his forehead, swallowed dryly. 'I got the right to be a tad uneasy, Harry. It's me who's been takin' all the risks while you an' Pegg sit back out of harm's way. Sorry, I know I ain't supposed to mention the man's name, but—' Tedder suddenly stopped talking, worried about going too far.

Grice pressed the steel into an expressive, rasping screech. At the explosion of bright, tiny sparks, Tedder wished he'd had the sense to have quit cold, instead of trying to explain.

The two men had met by the creek that connected a long line of shallow swamps, a mile or so out of town. It was called Lis Etang, but its name was long gone, along with the Cajun folk who had once lived there. No matter where you looked along its few miles' length, there was hardly an oak, tupelo or cypress to be seen. The boat loggers had decimated them. All that remained were stumps, and dark catfish holes. Where once local activity of the float camps kept the sawmills at Port Neches busy, there was now a silent, ghostly wasteland.

Fifty miles to the north, and heading west, a spur of the Gulf Railroad transported barrelled turpentine from the plant at De Quirrel. It was where Tedder had worked the local bayous, employed as an overseer of boxers and cutters. And he wished he'd stuck to it, instead of allowing himself to get involved with Harry Grice and the man he wasn't supposed to mention, Morton Pegg.

He'd caught their attention after he was upgraded to the company's stump blaster, started by accepting payment for running errands, occasionally leaning on those who wouldn't do what Mr Pegg wanted. But as time went by, Tedder found himself handling more dubious assignments, when the leaning got to be more forceful, and now he wanted out.

He knew the morning wasn't far away when he'd wake up to find himself surrounded by hunting dogs. He was paid well for what he did, but it wasn't ever going to stop the marshals from Lafayette.

I could go now … just disappear, he thought, watching Harry Grice put a needle tip to the slim blade. *I could take a train to El Paso … be safe enough there. I could keep my mouth shut about everything that goes on here, goddamnit.*

Grice's silence was now getting on Tedder's nerves. 'Are you listenin' to me, Harry?' he demanded. 'It could've been someone gettin' flushed out. Could've been me they were after. Hell, it's certain I'll get informed on one day. They can't pin everythin' on them bayou folk.'

Tedder's consideration was a realistic one. Recently, he'd been called on to visit certain people who, for one reason or another, had refused to do business with Pegg. He'd had to get tough with them until they changed their minds. He claimed there was an accidental death, but friends and family who found the body wouldn't have seen it that way, and neither would the law. 'I'm thinkin' of movin' on,' he added.

By now, Grice had decided he'd done enough honing. He took his foot from the iron treadle, slipped the knife into a leather sheath and looked up towards a cluster of dilapidated buildings. They were the abandoned sheds used for rosin and pine oil extraction.

'You know somethin', Tedder?' he said, telling rather than asking.

'Yeah, I know plenty. That's my ace in the hole, so to speak. I was gettin' round to it,' Tedder replied, knowing it wasn't what was meant.

'Your goddamn bellyachin's got me real worried.'

Tedder's shoulders sagged and his face lost a shade of colour. He was tough enough, physically strong and looked it. But Harry Grice was dangerous. His knife and high-priced Colt revolver weren't worn for effect; they were tools of his trade.

'Why should that be?' Tedder asked.

'Well it ain't so much *me*, old friend. It's *you* worryin' about *him*.'

It took a moment for Grice's reply to take on meaning, then Tedder turned to look behind him.

The short, dark-suited figure of Morton Pegg stood beside one of the old stump grinders. He was staring directly at Tedder.

'What the hell's goin' on?' Tedder grated, slowly backing off several steps, looking to the left and right of where Pegg was standing. 'How long have you been there?' he asked anxiously. 'I was just thinkin' about givin' somewhere else a try. There's no law against that, is there?'

'No, Winge, there isn't, but it's not *you* I'm worried about,' returned the level voice. 'It's all the stuff you're moving on *with*. You understand the concern that gives me, Winge. What a thorny position I'm suddenly placed in.'

'If you mean information, I wouldn't ever get to blabbin'. I'm implicated ... be diggin' my own grave.'

'What do you think, Harry? Do you trust him?' Pegg asked.

'It's a sword above our heads. Don't think I could live with that,' Grice warned.

Tedder trembled with tension as the ensuing quiet held and lengthened. He realized that Pegg had been there all along, had heard everything. Right now, the man was wondering if he could take the risk of letting him go – whether to give Grice the nod.

Tedder backed towards his horse. 'So you've heard my mind's made up. I guess what you do about it's up to you,' he said with bravado he didn't feel.

Grice drew his Colt, staring at the gleaming blued steel as though an old friend had arrived.

Tedder couldn't swallow; his mouth and throat turned arid. *It was how those people must have felt*, he thought. The not knowing, your very survival determined by others. The condemned man suddenly became aware of his surroundings, the cloying smells of damp timber and pine oil, the floating vegetation on old holding ponds. He cursed, heeled short spurs into the belly of his horse.

Harry Grice turned. Holding the movement of his Colt smoothly, he actioned the trigger and squeezed, just the once. A man with his gift wasn't going to miss from thirty feet.

Tedder gasped at the hammer blow between his shoulder blades and knew he was dead. *I didn't think he'd do it in cold blood*, he thought. *I should've kept my mouth shut.*

Jack Rogan didn't like being tricked. It was something that didn't sit well with a one-time professional gambler. He'd rather someone come right out and give you the bad news. It saved time before reading it in their faces.

What didn't make sense was what Gaston Savoy hoped to gain. In return for his life and the return of his belongings, Jack would give some sort of advice in the art of civil propriety. Goddamnit, Savoy could just as well tie him to a tree for his dogs to take chunks out of. From Savoy's standpoint, what sort of cockeyed return deal was that? Jack wondered.

'You know what I mean, Rogan,' Savoy started to explain. 'The day-to-day stuff, like, when to lift your hat; who gets the right o' way on the street or the sidewalk. When's it okay to curse an' blaspheme.'

Jack wondered again if Gaston Savoy was playing some cruel game with him, whether the moonshine was from a particularly muscular batch.

'I reckon you've already got someone,' he said. 'I heard them telling you not to wilfully kill just because you like it ... because you've no argument. That's a start.' Jack also thought there might be personal gain from Melba's little truism.

His uncertainty must have shown, for Savoy pressed him with another snort from the liquor crock. While Jack tried not to gag on the fiery liquid, Savoy stomped around the room, his language going in and out of a curious patois. It seemed to Jack as though the man was trying to convince himself that ignorance and poverty wasn't good fun after all.

'You got to see it from my side,' he said intently. 'We've been in this neck o' the woods for nearly ten years ... cut off for the most part. We've got along with our own way of life, but the world's changin'. I know, I've seen it. So, I reckon there's some o' my people who should have the chance to go along with it ... start livin' like regular folk, not goddamn swamp vermin.'

Savoy broke off at Jack's obvious incredulity. 'What's with the sneery look?' he asked with a harder edge to his voice. 'You think because we're from the bayou, we'll never get accepted as other folks' equals? Well I'm sayin' we will, mister, an' you're goin' to help us do it, lock, stock an' goddamn liquor barrel.'

Jack couldn't begin to see how, even if he wanted too. But he made a pensive expression and nodded, bided a bit more time. 'Well, if you're that set, an' I don't have a choice, there's not a lot to consider,' he said.

'There. What you just did. That's what I'm talkin' about,' Savoy almost shouted, pointed a big finger.

'What did I do?'

'Mopped your chops on your sleeve. *We* use the back of our hand, then lick what's left. Hell, Rogan, I swear, you're the one to learn us. You ridin' in here was an act o' divine providence. I'm thinkin' you was sent to convert ol' Gaston Olivier Savoy into a blue-chip, blue-blood. Goddamnit, no one's goin' to snigger behind our backs any more.'

'Steady,' Jack said flatly. He wanted to correct Savoy's idea of him riding in, but couldn't see the point. 'You're getting ahead of both of us,' he offered instead.

'Besides, I've been most places twixt here and the Mississippi. We both know it's not fair words or gentility you need.'

Savoy gave Jack a questioning look, inclined his head slightly as if prepared to hear more.

'So, I'm thinking all this isn't for anyone other than *you*. It must be something to do with Blackwater … why I'm your divine providence,' Jack continued. 'There's no one else here now, so if I'm right, tell me. I wasn't exactly the town preacher, but maybe I *can* help, instead of pretending to.'

'You know the place. Enough to know what's required of us.' Savoy extended a massive paw, relieved Jack of the crock. 'I'll need this when I'm finished,' he gruffed, his black eyes gleaming. 'I remember the first time I saw her. Up until then, I always thought Melba on a Sunday was a pretty enough sight.'

'Her? Who are we talking about?' Jack asked.

'Beatrice. The woman I fell in love with ten years ago.'

'What happened?'

'Someone else saw what I saw. He was some sort o' town official … took flowers an' fine manners an' a silver tongue. I never stood a goddamn prayer.'

Jack was intrigued, despite himself. 'And you've not moved on … wanted to?' he pressed.

'I want some o' what that goddamn cock-a-doodle-doo had,' came the brisk response. 'An' in case you're wonderin', my wife was already dead. She died soon after Melba was born. Look, Rogan, let's cut this drunken jawbone an' get down to cases,' Savoy continued after a short, fitting silence. 'I want to go back there … take the families with me. You understand?'

'Because of something that did or didn't happen ten years ago? Not really.'

'Not just that. But maybe. I'm not too sure. Hell,

I couldn't even fill out a docket for one o' them catalogue women. I couldn't do much anythin' with folk sniggerin' behind my back … urchins chasin' me down the street yellin' "hog boots". I got to be able to mingle with folk without soundin' like some goddamn foreign person. You can learn me if you're wantin' your horse an' that fancy pistol back, Rogan. Do you understand *that*?'

'Yeah. Though I'll be doin' it for *me* not you,' Jack retorted. 'I think there's a church schoolhouse in Blackwater. Maybe I could get you a bench there. It's where most learning starts.'

Savoy grinned and shook his head. 'An interestin' thought, but I don't have the time,' he said with a short, humourless laugh.

'How about I turn you into a gambler?' Jack suggested wryly. 'You'd intimidate most pikers into folding on anything above a pair. I'm sure it's not what you had in mind, but it's what I know about.'

'I've already told you, I want to go beside others. I don't want to be an outcaste 'cause o' manners or appearance. An' I'm speakin' for all of us. You know Blackwater … what's needed.'

'Yeah, I know what's needed. *That's* something different,' Jack muttered. 'You want me to create a falsehood. What if I said it's impossible and I can't help?'

'Then *I* couldn't help *you*.'

'What does that mean?'

'I'd let someone else decide what's to become o' you. Someone out there, who you've already done harm to.' As he spoke, Savoy leaned forward, pushed the door open a few inches.

The first person Jack saw was Melba. She was nearby, putting out eel traps at the water's edge. And Homer Lamb hadn't gone far. He was leaning against the bole of a tupelo keeping an eye on Savoy's shack. It looked like he was ready to bite himself with meanness. A number of men still seemed to be hanging around. Jack couldn't help but notice they were not only similar in looks and demeanour; their slouch hats, gunny-sack clothing and simple boots gave them the appearance of a makeshift, Territorial Army. To a man, they looked impatient to inflict a severe beating on someone.

Half-wit defectives, Jack silently accused. He'd bested a few of them and they shared a serious grudge. They would skin him alive if he was to tell Savoy that most of them would have been slaughtered at birth if they'd been bred as domestic livestock. 'Your threat's good enough,' he said. 'And have you got any kind of physic in here? My head's fit to blow apart.'

'I'll get Melba to feed you some willow wood,' Savoy offered. 'It works for *us*.'

6

The wind was soughing through the cypress and drapes of Spanish moss, feathering the grasses and bankside reeds. Around the Whistler township, birch lanterns glowed from flimsy cabins and a lonely dog yowled at the big moon.

The stillness and peace wasn't how Homer Lamb wanted it, not this night, anyhow. He'd lost status when Jack's horse chomped his fingers, and Jack had smashed him in the mouth. Now he sought retribution, wanted to harm Jack until he was beyond begging for mercy. Then he'd whip his ass across the bayou just to set things right.

But instead of being on the receiving end of Lamb's wrath, Jack Rogan was being entertained in Gaston Savoy's home. 'Probably bein' fed gumbo an' greens by Melba,' the man mumbled through a split lip.

Casting wary eyes at Lamb, Cletus Savoy was sidling around. He too was wondering if old Gaston had lost his edge. 'Fallin' for deceiver words,' he muttered darkly.

'Yeah. Looks like he's gone to fish from the far bank,' was how Loop Ducet agreed.

For almost a decade, the bayou people had weaved in and around Whistler with their hard, stubborn customs. Customarily, they dealt with those who came looking for trouble, in such a way there was hardly ever a return for more. They were a law unto themselves, made their own rules. But, if truth be told, there was never a time when anything else was needed. If towners considered them ignorant and rough-grained, they would live with it. 'Our strength is our family. What we have we hold,' Gaston was once fond of telling them.

But times were changing. There'd been talk of moving near to, even *into* Blackwater to live cheek by jowl with these townspeople.

'I've heard there's places where a man's not free to tote his own gun, or knife, or fishing pole, even,' Ducet protested.

'Yeah, an' the first time you used your rope would be to wrap it round your own scrawny neck,' Lamb put in. 'But *you'll* be all right, Cletus,' he added. 'Now you ain't got *nothin'* to get caught with.'

Cletus Savoy didn't smile or make comment. He wasn't sure if Lamb's remark was funny or serious.

*

Gaston Savoy's idea of conciliation with progress, was putting some men's nerves on edge, and their tempers were fiery. To Homer Lamb, the current business between Savoy and Jack Rogan felt like the last straw. Savoy was sharing a jug like they were old friends, a long, wet toast to carving up a future.

The thing Lamb was nervous and worried about, more than any alliance between Savoy and Jack Rogan, was a resettlement, a move away from Whistler. For a long while his dream had been to take over from Gaston Savoy as family leader. That included the women he wanted, all the power and authority he craved and the freedom to enjoy it. 'Gator in a pond o' bluegills,' was how he saw himself. A removal to Blackwater would change all that. Over time, the bayou clans would transform into respectful users of sidewalks, customers of stores with fancy goods.

It was enough to make a man spit, and Lamb did that just before flexing his shoulders aggressively and slouching off to the cookshack. He was nervy dry, thought snake-head would help him to stir those who would throw in with him.

Loop Ducet was of similar mind. He emerged from the shadows of the storehouses, nodded and jerked a thumb over his shoulder. 'I've already talked to some of the boys,' he said, with a sense of Lamb's intent.

'What about?' Lamb's voice wasn't loud, but it was

raw-edged, short with anger.

'They don't like interlopers an' poke-noses. Makes 'em feel kind of uncomfortable.'

'Good. We ain't family for nothin'. Huh, 'cept young Cletus, maybe. I'm worried about him. He ain't even ornamental.'

'You go too far with that ribbin', Homer. One mornin' you'll wake to your goddamn throat bein' cut, family or not. Serious. Don't you reckon Gaston's rubbin' our beaks in it … cosyin' up to that showboat tinhorn?'

'Even if I did, it's him callin' the shots. The head man can do what he likes. That's the whole point, Loop. If it means makin' a squinch-eyed fool of himself an' lettin' himself be taken for a sucker, then that's how it's goin' to be. Time bein'. You understand?'

'Yeah, I think.' Ducet studied the bigger man intently. 'What about that fat lip you got? An' what about Melba? I bet Gaston's got her mewin' an' stuff.'

'Feisty talk don't get the pot boiled, Loop.'

'What? You say I'm talkin' too much?'

'Don't mind a feller talkin', Loop, so long as it's the same feller backs up his words.'

'You want *me* to do somethin' about Rogan?'

'Not necessarily,' Lamb said, looking towards the chinks of light from Savoy's big cabin. 'I'm sayin', if somebody *was* makin' a move, they wouldn't be runnin' off at the mouth about it.' Lamb pulled down the brim of his hat, half turned away from Ducet. 'If anythin' was to go wrong, you'd end up sleepin' with the cottonmouths.'

'You got somethin' planned. I knew it,' Ducet said quietly.

But with his jaws grinding, Lamb was already walking away. He went behind the cookshack, peered out to the pole corral where a big sorrel gleamed in the darkness. He grunted, pulled the .44 Walker Colt from its holster and checked the loads. His disposition was growing hostility. He was ready to make his move, make the change.

After having watched her father chew on his corn dabs, Melba raised a tight smile at the thought of him tackling the basics of town conduct. Gaston Savoy had travelled to Baton Rouge and New Orleans, but that was all for taking notice of, not for fitting in. That came later, when he got home to Whistler.

'You act like any stranger in a new town, who plans to stay more than a night,' Jack Rogan was advising. 'Don't say too much, and don't make a noise. Don't spit or puke on the boardwalks, and nod courteously when someone in a dress goes by. It's probably a lady,' he went on. 'Take a bath and clear the pig muck off your boots.' He wanted to tell the old patriarch that he'd met toe chiggers with more style, certainly better taste than any goddamn Savoy. But, at that moment, his life depended on finding more accommodating words. 'And staying clear of the cat house and saloon's probably a good idea. Keep that up for a month or so, and who knows…?'

'An' what if we tire o' the kowtowin' an' eatin' their dust?' Savoy asked. 'Some o' the younger ones might not stick to it.'

'If it's thinking you have as much right as anybody else to be there … remember the Choctaws. It weren't so long ago, and *they* were clans, too.'

'Anythin' else?'

'Yeah, keep your dogs out of town. And look out for the law. It won't be wearing a badge of office, but it's there in some guise or other. Don't cross it.'

Responding to Savoy's notion of social integration, Jack was pitching somewhere between difficult and ludicrous. He thought he was getting away with it, enough to keep him alive that much longer.

He didn't like Gaston Savoy, yet there could be no doubting that the man was of extraordinary influence. Not by size alone did he control the fifty or so citizens of the Whistler settlement. He was the accepted chief, with his own order of bayou lifestyle. But while most other men in his position would settle for that, Savoy was going for more, including what he thought he'd missed along the way.

'You'll never pass for a West Point graduate, but with luck and a fair wind, you might just pass,' Jack said. Although he was thinking, *Not that it matters to me. I'm short in this goddamn hole. Time to get back where I belong. And no more short cuts.'*

By the same time tomorrow, Jack wanted to be sitting on a train headed East. Frog Hollow and the life forms of Whistler would ultimately merge into a tired traveller's old windy.

'I've learned that time's not for wastin' … to find out fast,' Savoy declared. 'I know what I want, an' hell-fire, I'm goin' for it.'

Yeah, that's right, feller. You and me both, Jack silently agreed. He was thinking that if he could mete out some measure of harm on his departure that night, it would justify his helping Gaston Savoy.

Without Melba or her father noticing, Jack lowered his head, peered out through a split in the cabin wall. From what he could see, there were few people about, and his eye sought out the picket line. There was a faint post light at either end, and Jack guessed his sorrel was there, wondered if anyone was watching out for it. He imagined the big horse wide-eyed and distrustful, ready to kick or bite a stranger, hoping he was going to turn up and get them away from there.

Yeah, I am … won't be long, lady, Jack said to himself.

He'd noticed how the swampers looked at his horse. They might be ill-bred, as thick as john seats, but they recognized horseflesh when they saw it. Jack had been offered heaps of dollars for the sorrel. But as long as the horse outran anything else on four legs, had more intelligence than the Whistler collective, there wasn't a price tag. Until it happened along, Jack thought it was only cowboys and troopers who admired and felt genuine affection for horses. Consequently, he wouldn't be leaving other than by an encouraging heel to the mount's muscular rump, and heaven help any hostile cracker who stood in their way.

'All right, Pa, that will do for tonight. We don't want to give that ol' brain o' yours a hernia,' Melba said, and Jack came back from his thoughts. 'He's done more learning this night than in his entire life. With prospect, he'll be more tuckered than one o' them Mississippi steamer girls. Ain't that so?' she added, with a challenging glance at Jack.

'There's towns out East where you get cast out for that sort of talk,' Jack replied.

'As you do for being a slick-fingered, card sharp.'

'Cut it out, you two. Is that sort o' smart talk an off-put with decent folk?' Savoy grated.

'I reckon so,' Jack replied. 'I've almost forgotten decent folk exist.'

'Your contempt for the likes of us is like a lit torch,

Mr Rogan,' Melba accused.

'It was the likes of *your* goddamn degenerate family that brought me here,' Jack snapped back. He strolled to the door, looked at Savoy angrily. 'Do I need your dog soldiers to show me back to that provisions store?'

'There's nowhere else for you to go. Not that's out o' harm's way. So don't try an' run off, Rogan. There's more murderous varmints out there wanting blood than you'll ever imagine.'

Jack caught sight of Melba's reproachful glare as he stepped out into the dark night.

'I can't imagine doing it on foot,' he said, wincing at the intimate cacophony of unseen croaks, ticks, barks and hisses.

He paused for a moment, looking back to Savoy's cabin. Melba seemed a cut above the rest, he thought, especially in looks. A bit of an enigma ... something from her mother's side. It was Melba who had given her father the idea of making use of him, seeing if there was anything to learn instead of turning him loose as quarry for the dogs. For that, he supposed he should be showing some sort of gratitude. 'Huh, think again, sugar pie,' he muttered. But he couldn't understand why she should be so hostile towards him, something out of nothing. He hadn't touched her, and she was certainly smart enough to acknowledge that if she wanted to. None of it altered the fact that she was just as much a primal threat as any other Savoy and, to Jack, represented just as much danger.

As he headed for the forage store, picking his way cautiously across the open ground, he took in that there really was no one performing any kind of lookout. He knew they were thereabouts, though, could almost smell them, feel their feral presence. Too bad he wouldn't have time to hand out a severe pasting to one and all, a real settle up for what they'd put him through. *Perhaps one of you will get in my way,* he was thinking as he entered the store.

He made plenty of suitable darkness and unfamiliarity noises, grunted noisily before pushing aside a vertical plank at the rear of the store. He bent low and shuffled out, for a long minute stood silently in the darkness, listening. Then, in the deep shadows at the back of the dilapidated sheds and store rooms, he moved towards where he knew the settlement's stake line ran.

Bitch lamps burned low and feeble at either end of the line of picket pins, but there was no one standing watch. Jack smirked. 'I guess even pigs get their heads down when they're tired,' he whispered to no one. Stepping across curls of strewn fodder, he walked the line. He expected to see the big sorrel standing impatiently between the swampers' mules, but he was disappointed and cursed silently.

They've moved her. That's why there's no one here, he thought. *It's Lamb. He's put her in his goddamn corral.*

Jack should have known that Homer Lamb would be ready for him when he tried to escape. So, much more alert now, he made his way to the pole corral he'd noticed earlier. Moments later he saw the sorrel, couldn't miss its size and shape. He was about to raise his hand in greeting, when he sensed the run of cold sweat between his shoulder blades. It was an instinct born of high-stake card games, treacherous adversaries and friendless places.

He turned to see Homer Lamb glaring at him from the shadows, his fingertip squeezing against the trigger of a big old .44 Walker Colt.

'Got you,' the man mouthed.

Jack knew it was the truth. This time he was facing his demise. It was there in Lamb's painful grin, the vindictive eyes.

Jack released his breath. He had allowed his mind to get scrambled in the last hour, only thinking of himself, his escape, the means. But there was always going to be someone laying for him, the one who'd been hurt most.

Homer Lamb was inferior to Jack Rogan by most reckonable gifts, but he'd outplayed him now and was going to do the cashing in.

With a knot in his vitals, Jack watched the fire-flash

from the chamber of the Colt. It was close range, but even as the gun blast shattered the night, his reflexes had already moved him.

There wasn't time for Jack's brain to transmit the message to his body and make sense of it. It was the instinct for survival that took him aside. A reflex action in a fragment of a second as Lamb's bullet cleaved his cheek.

Lamb was dragging back the hammer, getting ready for his next shot. But with a raging blood surge, Jack was no longer a soft, unmoving target. He suddenly became the most dangerous opponent Homer Lamb had ever faced.

Knowing that within seconds, Lamb's cronies would be gathering, Jack had little time. He lunged under the second shot, took a step forward, driving his forehead like a battering ram into Lamb's belly. As Lamb doubled up, Jack jerked the back of his head up, crunching the man's mouth shut with a vicious, jaw-breaking crack.

Dazed and staggering, Lamb dropped his Colt. He crumpled to the ground, unable to move or make a sound. Jack went for the big gun, but gasped when the toe of Cletus Savoy's boot connected with the side of his head.

Jack realized there were three of them as he held himself on his hands and knees. Shivering with revulsion, he recalled Gaston Savoy's warning about night critters, and didn't want to stay down longer than he had to. He wasn't going to let the next savage kick that came from Loop Ducet break his arm, either. He was mindful that it wasn't the blade of a knife or a rope around his neck.

'Not enough,' Jack railed. 'It'll take more than anything you gutless cow-heads have got. And there's nothin like a dose of desperation to get me up and going.'

He rolled from the impact of Ducet's boot, the swing of Cletus Savoy's scattergun. Then he turned again to Lamb, ramming his kneecap hard into the side of the man's face.

'How many more times, scumsucker?' he rasped. 'You won't have a mug left.'

Lamb was down and stilled, but Savoy and Ducet were on to him. Jack had his face rammed into the soft, dark ground, felt it filling his nose and mouth. He gagged, heard his ribs crack from another brutal kick.

But it wasn't his ribs which made the noise, he realized through the pain. It was the poles of the corral. He twisted his head, and through one eye and against the moon, he saw the sorrel rearing. Then the big horse was kicking free of the corral, bringing down its front legs, pounding its hoofs into the narrow back of Cletus Savoy.

'That's good. Kick the goddamn frost out,' Jack gasped. He was straightening up, wondering what to do next when somebody punched him in the back of the head.

7

Gradually, as though in slow motion, Jack staggered to stand straight. *Am I up?* he was asking himself. *Maybe I'm still down. Maybe, finally, I've got to be dead. But I'm not*, he reasoned. *They've been told not to kill me.*

He put a hand to his head where he'd been hit and turned around, immediately got a smack in the nose from a massive, tightly bunched fist. Fortunately for Jack, there was no intended follow through, and the punch only hurt, didn't down him.

'All gamblers lose in the end. No one ever tell you that?' Gaston Savoy's voice echoed across the dark swampland. 'But you're smart enough to know I'm not goin' to kill you. Lyin' on your back with a broken head won't get us anywhere.'

Yeah, lucky old me, Jack was thinking as Savoy grabbed him by the lapels of his coat. This was nearer the real Savoy; not so much the man who would be Mr Wellborn, but the roughscuff who regulated with his fists.

Something rammed painfully into Jack's stomach and he knew it was Savoy's forefinger, buried almost to the knuckle.

'Iffen that boy croaks, then you'll be followin' soon after,' the man threatened.

Stopping himself from falling forward, Jack let himself rest against the enormous hand. He wondered if it was Homer Lamb who was going to die, before quickly realizing it was Cletus Savoy. Then he sensed the loneliness and futility of dying alone, still fifty miles from where someone would know him. What was the friendly warning of the liveryman in Blackwater? 'Go a long ways above the swamps, not through 'em. They ain't nice people in there.'

Jack dearly wanted to hand Gaston Savoy – any Savoy – one more final smack in the mouth, but he wasn't up to it. His head, legs and arms wouldn't work properly. There wasn't much he could do, save ominous thinking. He was too far into the unfeeling area to grasp that Melba had arrived.

'Do him any more harm, Pa, and you might as well kiss goodbye to that future you so badly want,' she warned Savoy.

'Shut it, Melba. Just for once,' Savoy replied angrily. 'The man's gone an' broke your cousin's back.'

'It was the sorrel, not *him*,' Melba stormed. 'You going to beat them both to death? You know there's people waiting for him. He told us, they'll bring peace officers if he doesn't get home.'

'There's a State line in between. We're in Louisiana not Texas.'

'Oh don't be so silly, Pa. You think that'll stop the Texas Rangers? If you kill him, we won't be going anywhere, let alone Blackwater. You want to risk it on all our behalfs?'

Jack began picking up the odd word here and there. He was confused, not able to understand Melba's stance. It sounded accurate enough. Perhaps it really was for the good, his immediate future.

'Nonsense,' Savoy blasted. 'You're soundin' like you're protectin' him for some reason. Why? You betrayin' us, girl?'

'No, it's *you*. You're betraying what you tell us by what you're about to do. If you'd only taken the time to listen to someone other than Homer, you'd know the horse was staked out. When Rogan showed, Homer tried to make it look like he was stopping him from escape. It's impatience that gathers unripe fruit, Pa. Don't accuse me. Maybe they're right.'

'They?' Savoy almost snarled back at his daughter. 'What the hell are they right about?'

Jack felt Savoy's attention back away from him, sensed a change in the order of things.

'What most everyone's too scared to say out loud,'

Melba continued. 'That you're slipping ... past your peak. That maybe someone else should be looking to take over. If you go ahead and put Rogan here in the ground, you'll be bringing the hounds of hell down on us ... handing over to a would-be heir, without him having to fight you for it. We'll certainly never get to that Happy Valley you want for us.'

Feeling a little more clear-headed now, Jack found himself wishing Melba hadn't mentioned anything about burying him, even with an account of its shortcomings. He needn't have worried, though. Gaston Savoy's temper had flared when he heard that Jack had tried to escape, that he was to blame for the sorrel kicking through the corral fence and making an invalid out of Cletus. But hard-boiled as he was, big Gaston wouldn't do in cold blood what he might do when running hot. And he had no desire to swing for doing it.

Savoy turned on the line of men at the rear of the cookshack. They had been tending Cletus Savoy, who occupied a makeshift bunk along the end wall.

'Eliot, I'm sniffin' somethin' here,' he rapped at his eldest son. 'Was it how your sister says?'

'Reckon so, Pa. Seems like Homer expected Rogan to make a break for it. He was kind o' layin' for him out the corral ... came down with a bad case o' not figurin' it proper.'

For a long moment it was silent in the cookshack. Then Savoy turned to Jack. 'So maybe Homer did go off half-cocked. He's sure goosy enough,' he conceded. 'But that don't excuse you from what happened to Cletus. Ever since he lifted that fat poke o' yours, you've had it in for him. There was no harm done, so's why'd you urge that big ugly brute onto him that way?'

Jack spat dryly. 'The horse didn't need urging. And it's no big ugly brute. He's got wits and is a thorough-bred, which is a lot more than can be said for most of you sons-of-bitches,' he declared in a voice he managed to carry. 'When he sees a whole pack of wretched low-lifes, throwing their weight around, he just ups and does what comes natural. A kind of four-legged paladin. When it's *me*, I guess he just adds a tad more vim. You understand that, Savoy?' Jack wasn't at all sure that winning an argument with words was a good thing at that moment, or that his strength of mind would save him.

Having rated Jack as out on his feet, with little to retaliate with, Gaston Savoy was taken aback. He flicked a glance at Melba, who was watching Jack with a look he couldn't read. He looked at his men, was irked that they too seemed stirred by Jack Rogan's grit. Then he turned back to Jack, faced him accusingly. 'I ease you from bad trouble, an' offer you a way out o' this problem you got. Hell, for a while there in my cabin, I even had you tabbed as a not-all-bad, white man.'

Savoy shook his head slowly and Jack wondered if he was going to learn of his punishment.

'Then, first chance you get, you try an' cross me up an' make me look bad in the eyes o' my men; the men who wanted you to get together with my ol' bullwhip.' Savoy continued his summing up. 'What am I supposed to do, Rogan? We're all bein' let down.'

Jack shook his head in disbelief. 'You've got a real warped way of seeing things, Savoy,' he said. 'Like a cheap politician on the stump. Say anything in the morning, if it gets you what you want in the afternoon. You're all piss an' wind, 'cause you're plum out of ideas of how to get what you want. And you didn't need *me* to make you look bad in front of your men … your family. From what I've seen and heard, you've already done a fair job of that yourself … still are.'

'Hah, this speechifyin's what I like, Rogan,' Savoy grated. 'I ain't sure it's kind compliments you're payin' me, but I like the sound o' the words. An' I ain't dumb enough to miss the chance when it comes along … might use some of 'em myself one day soon.'

'Well, I like *your* words,' Jack continued. 'Some could make a cadaver chuckle. With me lending a hand you want to reform yourself. Then, and after a decade, you sashay into Blackwater as a wronged paramour. And while that's going on, your people are getting instant respect. Well, it's all bunkum, Savoy. You'll never be more than a plug-ugly, inadequate barbarian. As much an outsider to them, as I am to you.'

'There you go again, Rogan. I know you're right, but I don't like the sound o' why. I just know it ain't good.'

'Your new partner's insulting you, Pa … treating you like a fool,' Melba cut in.

Jack turned. It was faster than he meant and he expected the pain in his head to be sharp. But it was bearable, and thinking he'd rework the setup, he took a few steps towards Melba. 'And there was me getting to think yours was the voice of reason,' he said. 'Hell, I should have known better.'

There was movement from one or two of the men. They moved away from Cletus Savoy's bunk, attempted to look menacing, but Jack disregarded them.

'I once knew a couple of sheriffs who worked like that,' he went on. 'One of them would punch your head and the other would hand you a cool, damp cloth. An hour later they'd reverse the roles. You never knew where the hell you were. They kept it up until you said what they wanted to hear. It improved their arrest and conviction rate. What's your motive?'

'I'm learning,' Melba replied with a raised voice.

Jack blinked. 'Learning? Learning what?'

'How to deliberate. Or is there some other word for it?'

Jack took a deep breath. 'I think maybe there is, yeah, but that's near enough. It's what regular towns-folk do on street corners,' he said. 'What *you* folk would use clubs and fists for.'

'And what's a paramour?' she added, knowing full well.

'Ask your pa. He's been one, even if he doesn't know it.' Jack then wheeled back to Savoy. There wasn't much future in sparring with the girl, he realized. Especially as she probably exchanged feisty comments with half the male population of the neighbouring swampland. And there were things he wanted to say to her father.

'Just listen to yourself, Savoy,' he said. 'You don't know what to make of most anything. You think that someone you've already described as a no-good card-sharp is going to turn you into a man of character? It's farcical.'

'You're still in there with plenty jawbone. Sayin' plenty, still gettin' nowhere.'

'I'll tell you where I've got, Savoy. I'm a law-abiding citizen riding through the trees, minding my own busi-ness, looking for a short cut home. Your misbegotten nephew lumps along and decides to steal from me. I don't like it and give chase, an' all you can do is act as though you've done the most magnanimous thing in the history of mankind by offering me a job.'

'You finished?' Savoy said.

'No. You've got the cut and habits of a bum and a crook, but you're spouting a lot of horsecrap about being just the opposite. You think you can prove it by shifting people into town as though you're some sort of latter day Moses. And that's where *you've* got.'

Jack paused with an input of knowing breath. He'd got close to touching the fact. The whole situation really was a farce and bunkum. Gaston Savoy might well want to become a towner and get back some primitive standing with Beatrice Marney, but that wasn't all of it. It was nothing Jack had seen or heard – more what he *hadn't*. Savoy wanted him for something else.

'Well, what now?' he said, knowing he might have an edge. 'Do you keep me here until they come looking? The folk I'm talking about will drag you to Texas if they have to. Kidnapping's a capital offence back there. One they hang you for.'

Savoy was catching most of what was being said, but his mind had wandered. Once again he was thinking about whoever or whatever it was that had engaged his emotions for ten years. Being noticed in Blackwater was the last thing he wanted until he found what he was after. And for that he needed Jack's participation.

'Tell you what I'll do, Rogan,' he said, shifting ground slightly. 'I ain't sure I believe all that guff about folk comin' from Texas to rescue you. It's about what someone in your position would say. So, forget what happened tonight. You ain't goin' anywhere 'cause my boys'll let the hound dogs run you up a gum tree. If that happens, you'll stay there for a week with the kids flickin' army worms up at you. So, for your own protection, we carry on doin' what we been doin'. Then, I'll give you your money an' your guns an' safe passage from the swamps. The horse'll be guarded day an' night, until then.'

'How the hell are you going to manage that?' Jack retorted. 'It's a fact that polecats and other low varmints sleep for at least sixteen hours a day.'

Savoy gave a slow, chilly smile. 'That's it, feller, keep up the lip. But the sorrel's where you're vulnerable … your heel of Achilles. An' that sortment o' words comes from a low varmint with no schoolin',' he scowled.

Jack sighed. His new thinking was, as far as Achilles heels were concerned, Savoy definitely had one or two of his own. 'There's no such word as sortment,' he replied. 'It's the kind of beefhead mistake that'll get you noticed.'

Gaston Savoy gave a short, considerate nod. He looked past Jack towards his men who were still milling about anxiously. 'Do what you can for Cletus. Pour some shine into him,' he told them. 'The rest o' you get the sorrel, an' remake the corral. Our Mr Rogan's changed his mind about goin' anywhere just yet.'

*

Early morning, Jack had just finished a plateful of fried fish and corn bread. The door of Gaston Savoy's cabin was propped open with a branch, and he was looking through the cat-tails to the lily pads, speculating on the possibility of escape. But wading across the bayous would mean leaving the sorrel behind, then drowning and being eaten by alligators, so he turned to the more pressing commitment.

'I've agreed to help, but I really don't know what the hell you want,' he told Gaston Savoy, with Melba listening. 'I don't even understand the circumstances. I'm a gambler. So what I know is that the odds against you passing yourselves off as gentlefolk are about the number here in your clan, to one. You got to go East to learn that stuff, or leave the swamp and start your own obliging town.'

'Tell us what you know, what you had to do to last in that town.'

'I already have. I lasted as long as it took me to smack down someone who ill-treated his dog,' Jack replied. 'He wasn't exactly a class specimen. From what I recall, he was so backward, and mean with it, he might have been a relative of yours.'

Savoy ignored the insult. 'Then give us a broad picture,' he said.

'I'm thinking of a way to twist the obligation. Racing cockroaches around the rim of a hot plate might be entertaining, but it doesn't have much going for it, even in a place like Blackwater. I can teach you how to play stud and draw, but you'll have to know how to sit in on games of seven-up or faro. And you won't be able to carry guns to shoot up anything that takes your fancy. Mostly guns are worn for protection. That'll be from the likes of Homer Lamb and Loop Ducet.'

Savoy curled his lip. 'I'll worry about them. The rest ain't so difficult,' he said.

'It might be,' Jack responded. 'They've got a new-fangled system of transacting goods. If you want something you pay for it. With real money, like nickels and dimes, sometimes folding stuff. If you don't get the hang of any of those things, you can end up in a place they call jail. And *that's* for the likes of your Cletus. Or someone like him,' he added quickly. 'Think about how you treat outsiders here in Whistler because that's what's going to happen to you, if and when you put a foot in the wrong place. If it's integration you want, just do it, for Chris'sakes. Use politeness and civility. Look and learn. Pay your way.'

'We've got money,' Melba confirmed.

'Yeah, an' more comin',' Savoy agreed. 'Show us what to look for … what to learn.'

'I can win a hand of cards easy enough. But I don't reckon it's that talent you're really after.' Jack thought he was pushing a best guess for Savoy's purpose as far as he could. 'I'm thinking there's something you're not coming across with. Maybe a lot. What is it?' he said.

'Huh, you an' your thinkin' … your goddamn questions,' Savoy blustered. 'Hell, just get on with what we been doin', only more so.'

'What's your hurry?' Jack asked. 'I mean, I know what mine is.'

As though he had something on his mind and not certain whether to come out with it, Savoy stared at Melba for a moment before he spoke.

'The railroad workers are strikin' camp. They're moving on to somewhere in Texas an' we're takin' over their whole goddamn city. It ain't that far out o' town, an' if tent lodgements are good enough for them, it's a good enough start for us.'

'Like a fifth ace in a poker deck,' Melba started. 'I had no idea.'

'I was goin' to tell you. I had other stuff to think about.'

'But what's with the timing? We don't usually rush into anything.'

'If we're not there to keep an eye on them celestial heathens, they're likely to run off with what's bought an' paid for. We've got a week to get civilized,' was Savoy's final word.

8

Ten days later, it was a warm, quiet day in Blackwater. On the shadowed front porch of the High Chair Saloon, rambling honeysuckle dappled the light that fell across its weathered benches.

The popular, well-patronized saloon had recently become a hangout for a group of men who carried prominent Colts and proddy temperaments. Most of them were in the pay of the railroad, the lumber company or the town mayor.

There was no formal leader of these ill-tempered men, but Harry Grice saw himself as such, and no one was yet moved to challenge him. He was Morton Pegg's henchman who had forged himself a reputation with his fists and gun, occasionally his knife. The upshot was, whatever Grice considered worthy of his attention, others were similarly minded.

What grabbed Grice's attention now was the appearance of someone in the main street. The man was astride one of the unmistakeable mounts of Gaston Savoy, and as Grice stood up to get a better look, two men rose with him.

'Is that him?' one of them wanted to know. 'Is that Rogan?'

'Yeah, that's him all right. Jack Rogan,' Grice said, immediately turning towards the batwings.

'Where's *he* goin'?' another asked, as Grice disappeared inside the saloon. Then the man turned his attention back to the street. 'Interestin' feller by all accounts,' he added as the new arrival drew level with them. 'Out o' sorts lookin', though.'

'Probably a reaction to folks blowin' raspberries,' the other man suggested with a snort.

Meantime, upstairs on the saloon balcony, Grice was pointing out the rider to three of the most influential men in the county. Mayor Hockton Marney, Morton Pegg and the railroad tycoon, Benedict Bunce.

The men showed a keen interest as Jack rode by. There was a fascinating local rumour that Jack Rogan had been hired to put some kind of society polish on Gaston Savoy. But these men thought he might be something more. Maybe a gunsman.

'What do you think, boss?' Grice asked. 'You want him watched?'

'Later, maybe,' Pegg murmured. 'You don't ride into town unarmed, sitting a ploughboy mule if you're looking for trouble.'

Unconcerned about the interest he created, Jack rode direct to the telegraph office. He mailed a letter to his folks in Beaumont, Texas, but didn't tell them he was in a fix. He just gave them fibbery about his delay in getting home.

'I've seen you before,' the liveryman said five minutes later. 'Last time you had a good-lookin' sorrel. You sure come down in the world,' he added, with a meaningful look at the Savoy mule.

'Yeah. It seems a long time ago; I didn't take your advice,' Jack conceded with a wry smile. 'But it's not this animal's fault.'

After sorting out what was to be done with the mule, Jack was soon in the nearest dog hole bar. The small, canvas-fronted eatery was a remnant of the railroad workers, and he drank four shots of Pass whiskey, two before, and two after a bowl of biscuits and gravy. After being held against his will, he was taut and ready for a stretch. But he was bearing in mind the next few days, and decided to look around, try to estimate where there would be trouble for Savoy's when more than one of them made their way around town. He knew Melba was already there. It was no secret she was one of the Savoy clan's smartest. As such, she was getting on with integrating with the townsfolk in advance of others from Whistler who were moving into the tent camp.

Jack found her sitting on the porch of the Children's Orphanage. With another woman, she was handing out corn bread and milk. A wretched outcome of the railroad that had now pushed on further west into Texas was the abandoned offspring of its itinerant workforce. Curious as to her general intent, Jack took a quick look around him then crossed the street.

Melba stood up and smiled amicably when she saw him approaching. 'I was hoping to see you,' she said, and introduced the unhappy-looking lady as Elspeth Tedder. Melba explained to Jack that she was afraid that something had befallen her husband.

'It occurred to me that *you* could find out where he might be,' she said. 'He's disappeared. Just disappeared without a word.'

Jack wanted to say he knew how a close relative might feel about that. He appreciated that Melba was mindful of the irony, but now she was being expedient. It was a practical concern that wouldn't do her any harm in establishing herself in the town.

Elspeth Tedder explained that her husband had last been seen near the old holding ponds at Lis Etang. He was with two men, one of them definitely being Harry Grice. But since then, the man had claimed to know nothing about Tedder's disappearance.

'You can ask questions that we can't,' Melba said.

'And probably in places we can't go.'

Bearing in mind the feral character of Homer Lamb, Jack didn't think much for Elspeth Tedder's husband making a healthy reappearance. And, considering the animosity between himself and Lamb, he saw it as a possible, if not definite setback when all he wanted was a way out. He apologized and shook his head. 'I'm sorry, ladies. There's some personal stuff here, and right now it's not the sort of work I'm looking for.'

But just then he noticed one of the youngsters giving him an unnerving, unflinching look and he quickly changed his mind. 'Won't hurt to ask around, I guess,' he offered, curiously pleased when he saw Melba smiling back at him. 'I've got some places to go. Where's your pa?' he asked.

'The saloon,' Melba said. 'He's learning how to drink from a glass.'

Many of Blackwater's citizens had heard rumours about Jack Rogan and the Savoy clan. They had speculated at what had happened out on the bayous, and what was going on at the rail workers' camp. Now, towards the end of the day, they were having a close look at the mysterious stranger.

'He's leadin' 'em from their nether world,' one shopkeeper said, as Jack walked by.

'Whatever he's up to, he don't look too different

from any of us,' replied another.

When local folk saw men like Blanco Bilis or Harry Grice on the streets of Blackwater, they had no trouble recognizing them as drunken troublemakers or professional toughs who were best given a wide berth. But Jack Rogan didn't seem to fit either category. So far, he was a man holding his own counsel, returning their open scrutiny with a clear lack of concern.

As for the man himself, Jack was doing what he needed to do because he wanted his sorrel, his Colt and his $1,000 back. He wasn't working out a contract to hurt anyone, and didn't want it to look otherwise.

To him, Blackwater had only been one of many stopovers between the Mississippi and Beaumont, Texas. It was where the liveryman had advised him to go around the swamps, not through them. 'They ain't nice people, an' the land's crawlin' with 'em,' he'd warned.

It didn't take Jack long to check out the town's gambling ground. As he suspected, it was mainly contained within the High Chair Saloon. He had little doubt he could take most of its clients inside a week if he wanted. But he wouldn't be turning any cards or rolling any dice this night. All he was interested in was serving his time and getting the hell out. *So what are you doing seeking out those who'll likely respond very badly to being asked questions?* asked the voice inside his head.

Now he stood looking at the bright yellow light

shining from the windows of the saloon. On one of its outside benches, sitting at a table with a fat, tallow candle, Gaston Savoy was chatting enthusiastically with an attentive, well-dressed lady. Jack guessed immediately she was the one who'd given Savoy his marching orders a decade ago; the lady who'd gone on to marry an ambitious town official.

'Melba told me you'd be here,' he said. For a moment he wondered if he'd said the wrong thing, if the lady might be concerned about who Melba was.

Ah, what the hell, he thought, and offered an untroubled smile.

'Mr Jack Rogan, this is Beatrice Marney. We go back aways,' Savoy said.

Jack nodded and shook the lady's hand. 'How'd you do? Are we all newcomers?' he asked.

'No, Mr Rogan. I've been here for more than ten years. If the town hadn't already got itself a name, it could well have been Marney.'

'On *your* side?'

'No, my husband's. He's the mayor.'

Jack made easy talk for a minute before saying he had business elsewhere. 'There's much to be discovered in a new town,' he said. 'How the place operates, who pulls the strings. A lot of it should be starting up about now.'

'He's right,' Savoy granted. 'An' looking after a

big family takes a lot of work. Having moved on and all, folk seem real interested in what we're doing. Someone wanted to know what we were bringing to the Blackwater table. Maybe I should start to tell 'em.'

Jack smiled at the change in Savoy. Gone was the ignorant swamper, the hard-nosed clan leader from deep in the bayou. Suddenly the man was of considerate words, smarter appearance, a more thoughtful manner.

'It's interesting to hear what Gaston has to say about his family, his people,' Beatrice said, as if of similar thought. 'We're somewhat isolated here, don't really know much about the lives of folk from other parts. He paints quite a colourful and interesting picture.'

Hah, don't I know it, Jack thought. 'Perhaps one day he'll be running for office,' he suggested more light-heartedly. 'A delegate of the common citizen … the underdog, even. You'd best warn your husband, Mrs Marney.'

'Are you suggesting my Hockton spreads his concerns unequally, Mr Rogan?'

'I wouldn't know, would I, ma'am? It's just that in my experience, those that live off the land often have very little to represent. Two years ago, a judge asked an Arkansas dirt farmer why he robbed the local bank. The man's reply was, "because that's where all the money is, Your Honour". Looking at it with a squint, you can kind of see what he was getting at.'

'Can you?' Beatrice replied with an inscrutable smile. 'Don't leave just yet. I've asked my niece to join us for a drink. I'm sure she can shed some light on to the twilight activities of Blackwater. Play your cards right and she might even show you, if you ask nicely.'

'Hah, I can see you hittin' it right off, Jack,' Savoy joined in. 'Here, these are yours I believe. You must feel near naked without 'em,' he said, handing over a small sack.

Jack took it, knew what it was without looking. He just couldn't immediately fathom out why. Savoy still had his sorrel and his grubstake, so giving him back his guns was hardly setting him on the road to freedom. Maybe it meant he was close to what Savoy really had him in town for. *Makes more sense,* he thought dryly.

He put on his gunbelt and adjusted it, pushed the pocket revolver into the waistband of his trousers. Suddenly he felt a tad more secure than when he'd ridden into town. He had no interest in the personal business of Beatrice Marney and Gaston Savoy. He was asking about some of the town's night-time activities, when Beatrice smiled broadly and held out her hand.

'Lauren dear,' she said happily as her niece arrived. 'This is Gaston Savoy and Mr Jack Rogan.'

'How do you both do?' the woman responded to the introduction.

Jack, smiled at the economical response, the voice that sounded more Georgia swank than Louisiana swamp. *Luck's changing,* he thought, removing his hand from the stock of his Colt.

A quarter hour later, Jack was sipping coffee with Lauren Kyle in the lobby of the Blackwater Hotel. He indulged himself in eager conversation, talking of fashions on Mississippi riverboats, and amusing local patois for whiskey and beer. Lauren was a timely reassurance that not everyone between the Mississippi and Sabine rivers was coarse-grained and uneducated. He was totally unmindful of the passage of time, of what he'd meant to do before meeting Beatrice Marney's niece.

Jack's appreciation for Lauren was clear, and he thought reciprocal, after he had walked her home. He left her with an agreement that they would get together again. He wasn't certain when this would be – was hoping for sooner, because it wasn't likely there'd be a later.

He was walking back past the High Chair Saloon listening to the music spilling over the batwings before he remembered. He'd done nothing about Elspeth Tedder's disappearing husband, hadn't even thought about it.

The saloon was filled with raised voices and hearty laughter. The music of a mechanical piano tried to make itself heard through the spirited noise.

Harry Grice wasn't hard to spot. He was standing at the far end of the long bar flanked by several of his armed cronies. Jack weaved his way through the busy customers towards him, stopping momentarily when he saw the broad-shouldered man standing with his back to him was Homer Lamb.

He'd been surprised when Elspeth Tedder had mentioned Lamb's name in conjunction with Grice, but now he was thinking, why not? Their qualities were probably ideally suited. He continued a pace, turned to the bar and ordered whiskey.

Lamb either heard Jack's voice or noticed him in the back-bar mirror. He turned sharply, his face already darkening as their eyes met.

Jack raised his glass. 'Coincidence, or what?' he said. 'Why don't you introduce me?'

'I was introduced earlier in the day. You weren't,' Grice suggested. 'What do you want?'

Jack half grinned. Twisting the shot glass in his fingers, he leaned back against the bar. 'Fellow by the name of Winge Tedder. It seems you were the last person to see him before he went missing. So his wife's wondering why no one knows anything. I told her I'd ask.'

A nerve twitched under Grice's right eye as he took a step back from the bar. 'That's very good o' you,' he said icily. 'But nobody knows what happened to him. What are you suggestin'?'

'I'm not suggesting anything. I'd like to know from that "nobody", what happened.'

'You got a smart way with that mouth o' yours,' Grice said venomously. 'I can see why it's got you into so much trouble.'

Grice's cronies shuffled uneasily. Homer Lamb smirked, crooked his thumb around the sheath knife that hung around his shoulder. They were all clearly enjoying the verbal scrap, sensed it was leading to more.

'I told Mrs Tedder I'd find out what happened to her husband,' Jack said. 'You were seen with him near some old holding ponds. He wasn't noodling for catfish, so you just tell me what was going on, and there'll be no more of that trouble I get into.'

'That sounds to me like a threat, Rogan,' Grice responded. 'Now, you got a handful o' seconds to tell me you've made a big mistake. If you don't, you've a lesson comin'.'

Jack could see what was coming, but he wasn't unduly bothered. Grice was on the back foot, the talk was his thinking time – the gambler bluffing with a bum hand. Jack had tangled with that sort all along the Mississippi, and he'd always got the better of them. It came with the territory, one of the adrenalin-fired appeals of gaming for money. But it was also part of the life he was supposed to have turned his back on.

'For Chris'sakes, Grice, I just want to know what happened to him,' he snapped angrily. 'If you know something, tell me.'

Jack's demand was deliberately provoking. The smirk disappeared from Lamb's face. As he shuffled sideways, Grice's henchmen got away from behind him.

'I'm through talkin', feller,' Grice rasped.

The man had the speed of a hired gunman, but Jack was more prepared. The flash and resounding blast of a single shot filled the barroom. With one hand clutching his shoulder, Grice staggered back, cursing, as his gun clattered to the floor.

'That's why you don't see turkeys wearing guns,' Jack said. 'They're too slow by half. If I'd wanted, I could have put that bullet through your mouth.'

It was instinctive for Jack to swing his Colt to cover Lamb. But the big, bearded swamper made no move for his gun. He just stood there with his mouth hanging open, his dark eyes filled with loathing.

'If there's law in town, go get it,' Jack commanded, his words cutting the breathless silence.

Lamb worked spit around his mouth. He shrugged insolently, walked to the saloon doors like a man with short-lived allegiance.

9

By ten o'clock in the morning, the mayor already smelled of alcohol. He wanted another belt as he looked out from the balcony above the Gulf Railroad offices.

He had an uninterrupted view of the Whistler families, their flat-bed wagons, hand-carts, hogs and mules that were taking up residency at the Chinese railroad workers' tented pitch on the outskirts of town.

Until the past few days, Mayor Hockton Marney had had no concerns about the removal to Blackwater. It all made for an easier, trouble-free takeover of the bayou township, its occupant-free land. It was a venture which he'd been deeply involved with for months, but almost overnight, things had changed.

Although central to the deal, Marney had originally laughed at the notion of Gaston Savoy leading his swamper families to a promised land, giving them a voice for openness and equality. But now, the arrival of Savoy's forceful presence concerned him. With the upcoming elections, it could create a distraction he didn't need.

The two men had been foes ever since Marney won the hand of the woman they were both smitten with. In the ten years since, he had grown rich and powerful while Savoy lived out on the wetlands, relatively deprived and remote.

Unexpectedly, Savoy was now assuming the manner of a civic-minded resident of Blackwater and was putting himself around a bit. To make matters worse, Marney's wife had been seen drinking with Savoy, while he'd been busy elsewhere.

Marney thought there was more to it than just swampers moving into town. And he was taken aback at the lack of interest shown by his business associates. He let his gaze drop to the street below. A couple of passersby glanced up, but their acknowledgment appeared more courteous than friendly.

'Looks like these folk have suddenly got something on their minds,' he said, stepping back into the room. 'If I didn't know any better, I'd say they were giving themselves room for thought.'

'Well, you *do* know better,' Morton Pegg growled around a large Corona. 'You're creating something out of nothing, so stop chuntering on.'

'There's a fair number moved into that goddamn tent camp now, and Savoy's already got the ear of a handful o' townsfolk. Him and the girl, who's doing charity work,' Marney continued. 'Some of them are interested in what he's got to say, and that's how you start. Indifference is how you lose. I reckon the old goat wants to be someone. He's big and mouthy enough for them to listen.'

'For Chris'sakes, you have to get nominated for most anything in Blackwater,' Pegg said. 'Who do you reckon controls that?'

The railroad man was even less sympathetic. 'An' who cares about what *they* all want? Since when has an election stopped *us*?' Benedict Bunce was an educated man originally from the East, but he slipped easily into the railroad workers' argot. 'Goddamn towners. *I* think king's ransom, while *they're* thinkin' pig dirt,' he sneered.

'And that's not how I want to end up, Ben.' Hockton Marney was accustomed to success and prepared to do almost anything to ensure it continued. To that end, he'd become involved in a venture with Bunce and Pegg which, although not illegal, required certain illegalities to conceal its purpose. At the end of the day, he was as greedy as the timber man and the railroader put together. He just lacked their ruthlessness.

He drained the brandy, put the glass down and held out his hand, palm downwards. 'I'd never have made a gunsman,' he said, staring at the spread of his trembling fingers. 'So where do we go from here?'

'That's more like it, Mr Mayor.' Although of short stature, Morton Pegg looked every inch the successful entrepreneur with a three-piece suit and shiny black boots. 'The doc says the bullet ripped through the fat in Harry Grice's shoulder. He was lucky, but I doubt he'll be seeing it that way. I think this Rogan feller could have shot him anywhere he wanted,' Pegg said. 'Unfortunately, our straw sheriff won't press charges because every person standing close swore Harry was pushing for it. Even a few who weren't. Huh, such is his and our popularity, gentlemen.'

'I'll fire Buckmaster when I'm re-elected,' Marney promised.

'There you go, Hock. Seein' a future already,' Bunce said. 'But right now we got a problem with this Jack Rogan. He's more'n Savoy's side-kick, that's for sure.'

'How do you mean?' Marney asked uneasily. 'What sort of problem?'

'A prospective one. And that's the trouble.' Bunce leaned forward and banged the stopper back in the brandy bottle. 'Like Winge Tedder.'

A thin film of sweat glistened on the mayor's florid face. Although he'd had no part in taking out Winge Tedder, he'd known about it. That made him every bit as guilty as the others. A business killing was one thing; one with blood and a body was something else, not his kind of work.

Bunce saw Marney stare at the brandy. He reached out and lifted the bottle away.

'You've had enough,' he said. 'I hope you're not goin' to fall apart 'cause someone's said boo. You know we can't have a weak link.'

'Hell, Ben, give me a break,' Marney replied. He was shaking like an aspen. 'We all get a setback now and again. What were you saying about Rogan?'

'I'll tell you what we know about him,' Pegg said before stepping past Marney and out onto the balcony. The hard-driving timberman wanted Blackwater as *his* town, considered himself in a strong position to take it. But there was a ways to go and they couldn't afford to overlook any kind of threat.

Pegg turned around, back to facing the men in the room. 'I was told he tangled with the Savoys – knocked all sorts of stuffing out of one or two of 'em. Lamb says they've got his horse and his cash savings, that's why he stays, why he's helping 'em with whatever it is he's helping 'em with. But after last night, I'm not so sure. Who is he – what is he? A lawman? A gunman?' he continued.

Bunce fiddled with a silver trinket hanging from his watch chain. 'I heard he was takin' a detour through the swamps one dark night an' stumbled into a half-wit Savoy. That's what I heard, anyway.'

Marney and Pegg nodded concern and waited for Bunce to carry on.

'When the deal's done, I'll be movin' on, an' I don't intend to let anyone stop me, goddamnit. Last night, this Jack Rogan went up against our best muscle for info about Tedder. That makes him a sure-fire threat,' the railroad man declared.

'You got any ideas about what he's up to, then?' Marney asked.

'No. But what if he's some sort o' Pinkerton agent workin' undercover? What if he's been brought in by old Savoy to check us out? What if he's tipped him off about the goddamn timber? There's a whiff of something here I don't like.'

'Are you saying what I think you are?' Pegg said.

'Yeah, probably. There's a fortune waitin' out there for us, an' I'm not havin' some interloper put a spike in.' Briskly, Bunce pushed himself up from his big, office chair. 'I say we rid ourselves of him.'

'If you reckon that's the only way out, I'll second it,' Pegg said with a searching look towards Marney.

Marney managed a tremulous nod. What could he say? His requirements matched theirs, and there was no danger of going up against them.

Jack Rogan sat quietly in a cane-bottomed rocker in the lobby of the hotel. But his mind was active, brimming with schemes. His effectual jailer was strolling around town in his store-bought outfit, telling anyone who'd listen about how they were all looking forward to integrating. In between supervising the settling in of the first few families, Gaston Savoy had been impressing Beatrice Marney with his new and finer style.

Consequently, Jack realized that right now could be a good time to ride for Whistler. He could make another try at breaking out his sorrel, tearing Savoy's cabin apart, and anyone else's, until he recovered his $1,000.

Jack knew that Homer Lamb was in town, but now there was also Loop Ducet, Eliot and John Savoy, and a whole pack of nephews and cousins. There was a chance he *could* get his horse back without having to crack a skull, or worse.

That thought prompted him to recall last night's confrontation with Harry Grice. He doubted a flesh wound was ample enough warning for a hired gunhand. After getting his arm patched up, Grice was the sort of man who'd promise to settle the account, if only to himself. If there was a next time, there'd be no restrained message.

It was late afternoon and Jack went to stand outside the hotel. Within minutes, he'd noticed the change, the reserve of those townsfolk who passed by. They might still perceive him as a man who rides mules, but now it was different. Once upon a time Jack carried a reputation. He was a professional gambler who'd been known from Baton Rouge to Vicksburg as someone not to mess with. In Blackwater, Harry Grice was an intimidating individual, but Jack had taken him on, and put him down, publicly.

Jack was close to making a decision about what to do next when he saw the bright, red-painted wheels of a buckboard approaching. The vehicle slowed, swung towards the hotel when the driver saw him.

'Good afternoon,' Lauren Kyle, said unsmiling.

Jack tipped the brim of his hat. 'It is that, Miss Lauren. I like your buggy.'

'Hmm. Must say I'm a little disappointed in your choice of local amusement.'

'Keeps me off the street,' Jack flipped back. 'How did you hear about it?'

'*Everyone's* heard about it.'

'Well, you knew I was no storekeeper.'

Lauren studied him closely, her gloved hands in her lap, holding the reins. 'You're somewhat of an enigma, Jack Rogan. Gentleman one minute, ruffian the next.'

'It's probably the company I've been keeping,' Jack replied, not continuing with the smile.

'Maybe. However, I don't want to bandy words. I actually came to ask if you'd care for a drive along the river.'

'Well, I'm not sure about that,' he said, not meaning a word of it. He was about to say something about being seen with a ruffian, when he saw Melba Savoy heading his way along the boardwalk. She was beside the unmistakeable form of Homer Lamb.

The moment Melba saw Jack she clasped Lamb's arm, held it until they were up close.

'Miss Savoy,' Lauren said. 'Are you enjoying your stay in the big city?' she added sarcastically.

'Well, I *was*,' Melba replied coolly. 'And what about you, Mr Rogan? Are you enjoying the fishpots?'

'Yes, such as they are. And I think you mean, flesh-pots,' Jack corrected.

Melba smiled. 'I know what I mean, Jack. It's my pa who's short on words. I'm content with what I know.'

Lauren sniffed. 'Well, if you're staying here, Jack.'

'Rather than watch red foxes chase frogs in the twilight?' Jack climbed up into the rig to take over the reins. 'I wouldn't want to miss that.' He tipped his hat. 'You too have a pleasant evening, Melba.'

'There's dancing here at the hotel, later. Come on, Homer,' Melba said irately, tugging at Lamb's brawny arm.

'I hope you brought your clogs,' Jack said and winked playfully.

Homer Lamb couldn't understand his good fortune, the sudden warmth that Melba was demonstrating. But before he had time to more fully appreciate the offer, reality took over. Learning that Jack Rogan was on his way out of town, there was no way he could take advantage of the invitation.

Melba didn't understand when Lamb muttered an apology, a lame excuse, before hurrying off. When she realized she was cursing, she smiled and continued along the boardwalk.

10

Gaston Savoy was thoughtful as he headed towards the Blackwater Hotel. There were a few families settled into the tented city, and over the next few days there would be a few more, continuing until the move was complete. He was getting them settled in stages, hoping to avoid antagonism between his people and the unsuspecting townsfolk of Blackwater.

Casting a shadow over the mass departure was the fact that he hadn't yet got around to actually signing over Whistler and its surrounding land. All he'd received to date was the buyers' down payment, and most of that had gone to the Chinamen.

But Savoy was pleased with the way things were progressing; satisfied to see just how much a little learning and tidying-up had smoothed the course of integration. He was winning over people on a business and social level, laying down his plan for the future. It was a vision based on more equality, why no one should simply move aside for big business. And the folk of Blackwater had an ear for such talk.

A few men had made fortunes from the defilement of the bayous, huge tracts of land torn bare by the reach of the loggers. It was a business that Savoy fervently reviled. If any man lopped so much as a tupelo branch within striking distance of Whistler, he took his life in his hands. It was how Savoy's fearsome reputation had started.

By standing aside, Savoy could have made himself a fortune ten times over, and in as many years. But he'd stubbornly refused all such offers until the right buyer came along.

On his trip to New Orleans, Savoy met James Chester. The man represented the Department of the Interior, who were becoming interested in the preservation of the country's forests and wetlands. Chester struck Savoy as honourable and far-sighted, with commitment and deep pockets.

Savoy was selling out for an acceptable dollar, and he planned to use the money to re-locate and improve the lot of his people. Although he hadn't informed them of his contract with Chester, it had always been the reason to get moving. The signed deed had stipulated clearing the land of any settlement.

When Savoy had admitted to Jack what he'd done, the way he'd gone about it and why, Jack had dubbed him Don Quixote. Savoy responded with pleasure at the required explanation, said it was a make he was happy with. Most everybody commended him for what he was doing. Everybody that is, except the person he was most keen to impress.

Beatrice Marney had told him she thought he was making a mistake, that his way of thinking was rooted less in selflessness and more in his desire to be accepted by the people of Blackwater.

'Not just *them*, Beatrice. *You*,' he'd responded quickly. 'And what's so goddamn wrong with that?'

'You don't need to, Gaston. I see you as a strong, uncomplicated man who knows what he wants and leads by example. Or *used to be* at least. Now you're trying too hard ... bullying with your ideas and ambition. Like my husband used to.'

'Yeah, well perhaps if I'd been less backward ten years ago, you'd have married me.'

Beatrice shook her head at that. 'Do you want to know why I chose Hockton over you, Gaston?' she asked.

'I guess.'

'Because I was just like you. Style over substance, the legislators call it. I married the trappings of office, not the man, and I've regretted it ever since. Do you understand what I'm saying, Gaston? Over the years you've held your people together ... fought off what you don't want or believe in. I've come to admire you and your ways, but I'm fearful of what will happen to you – the price you're set to pay. Look what's happened to Hockton.'

'What? What's happened to him?'

Beatrice thought for a moment, looked disappointed. 'It's gone, Gaston. No need to explain. It's gone, that's all.'

Savoy could see what was meant. All ideas he'd had about him and Beatrice Marney were pie in the sky. There wasn't going to be any future together, agreeable or otherwise.

The patriarch of the bayou families halted in his thoughtful reverie. He sighed, put a hand against an upright at the edge of the boardwalk and took a long look around him. The moon was on the rise; affecting night scents from the mangrove were drifting in across the town.

Savoy had felt some reservation from the moment James Chester made him the offer for Whistler and its land. He'd been occupied by planning, now by implementing the big change from the old way of life to the new. He wanted to buy one or two new-builds on payment of the balance of Chester's contract. But, along with seeing Beatrice Marney again, it was true that the big man with the big ambitions hadn't taken much of a look at what he was doing.

Blackwater had grown fast on the back of its nearby timber, but with available tracts stripped bare, the industry had eaten itself up. The needy town turned its attention to other businesses, mainly the trade brought by the railroad, its connections to the Mississippi in the East and the Rio Grande to the West.

Standing there now, in the moonlit, peaceful silence, Savoy was acutely reminded of what he'd left behind.

Moments later he brought his mind back to the present. Since the shooting at the saloon, he wanted to reassure himself that Jack Rogan was staying clear of trouble. Jack's real help wasn't over yet, not by a long chalk. Savoy didn't want the man hatching any plans about running out.

'If I was the old Sabine Cuff, I could eat you alive, Pa,' the voice sliced through the darkness.

Savoy flinched, turned to see his daughter standing alongside him. 'Sorry, gal. I was just thinking,' he said.

'That's what you do before you leap.'

'I know. Have you seen Jack around?'

'No. Not since he went ridin' with Madam High-Hatty, Lauren Kyle,' Melba replied tartly.

'Oh. So that's why you got a face like one o' your squashes.'

'Huh. Good riddance to bad rubbish, I say.'

'Come on, Melba. You don't feel that way an' you

know it.'

'Well maybe not. Maybe I'm wishin' it on this place.' Melba glanced around like everything offended her. 'I've not known many towns, an' I guess I like this one least of all,' she said.

'We've had all this out more'n once, Melba. I hope we're not startin' back on in.'

'No, Pa. But that don't mean I understand it all. Like I haven't done ever since you came back from New Orleans. Have you stopped to think that, in between, we've all done what *you* wanted?'

'Yeah, I've thought on it, Melba. An' in time, they'll know I was right when their kids grow up with nobody lookin' down on 'em. You'll see.'

'I hope so, Pa. I really do.'

'I reckon there's somethin' else stuck in your craw, daughter,' Savoy pressed. 'Doin' good work, handin' out grub to the real poor an' needy's not what you're railin' against. Didn't you say you had a date with Homer, tonight?' he asked. 'I remembered, 'cause it's such a turn out. Where is he?'

Melba grimaced. 'It's hard to believe that man is actually related to any of us. I only said I'd go to the shindy with him to put Jack Rogan's nose out of joint.'

'Jack Rogan?' Savoy said in surprise.

'Yeah, him. You'd know if you'd been there. Anyhow, would you believe he walked off an' left me standing on the corner? Ha, Homer Lamb walked out on me. You reckon I'll live that down, Pa?'

'Of course. No one's goin' to believe *him*, are they? But I am wonderin' why he'd do such a thing.'

'Ten minutes ago, right after Jack Rogan drove off with Lauren Kyle. The minute they swung that rig around, he was up an' runnin'.' Melba paused to think a moment. 'Reactin' like that was kind o' strange. I mean, he hates Jack somethin' fierce,' she said with palpable concern.

Savoy stepped down into the street and looked towards the river, 'What the hell's all that?' he grunted broodingly at the muffled sound of distant gunfire.

The night heron that had been stalking young catfish was a long way from town. But it was still closer than the hunting fox had wanted to be. The scents and sounds made the animal nervous and watchful as it bent its bloodied muzzle over the still carcass.

Dragging its kill from the reeds of the shallow creek into bankside grass, it suddenly lowered its head and laid back its ears. There was no doubting its sharp senses; man wasn't far away, and was creeping furtively along the water's edge.

Troubled, the fox dropped its kill and turned away, ran swiftly towards the shadowed sanctuary of the old cypress stumps.

11

'Where in hell's name are they?' Blanco Bilis hissed.

'Not so loud. Your voice carries,' Harry Grice answered back through the moon-shadowed trees. 'Didn't they say anythin' about where they were goin', Homer?'

'Not that I heard. Rogan said something about watchin' goddamn frogs,' Homer Lamb growled. 'They wouldn't have gone much further than Lis Etang, though. There's nothin' to see beyond the creek.'

There was an uneasy edge to Lamb's voice. He was known as a man who feared little, but tonight was different. He had openly aligned himself with men who were opponents of Whistler, its families and its land. Now he was in up to his neck, and party to a hired killing.

'Yeah, let's move,' Bilis, said. 'There's critters here that only feed at night, an' you can't hear 'em comin'. Besides, I want to see what Rogan an' that chickabiddy's up to,' he sniggered.

There were four of them. Lamb, Harry Grice, Loop Ducet and a last minute Blackwater lout who would do anything for the price of a drink, Blanco Bilis. They moved on, their progress marked by the noise of the rise and fall of clicking beetles and croaking bullfrogs.

Earlier in the day, Grice had been told to take Jack Rogan out of the game. Knowing how Homer Lamb felt towards Rogan, Grice let on about the assignment. Lamb was surprised at its imminence, but when he saw Jack leaving town for a trip out to the bayous, he saw a timely opportunity.

Grice had a humiliating defeat to avenge and an assignment from Morton Pegg, so he hadn't wasted any time. With his left arm in a sling fashioned from an old bridle, he'd quickly gathered three ready and available guns.

A thin carpet of mist settled across the stagnant pools of water as they approached the old lumber workings of Lis Etang. Moonlight glinted on their assorted gun metal, but Grice assured himself there was no way they could be seen or heard, other than by small and timid night critters. He peered into the gloom around him. 'Must be around here somewhere,' he said louder than he meant.

'What? What's around here?' Bilis asked anxiously.

'It's where they should be. Rogan an' the girl,' was

the reply after the shortest moment's hesitation. But Grice's mind had wandered. He'd been speculating on which stagnant waterhole held Wenge Tedder's body, if it had been eaten by mudbugs or hauled away by an alligator.

A hundred feet distant, Jack Rogan knew nothing of the grim-faced men who were hunting him down. But he had seen what he thought was a startled fox. It was jumping the dark, catfish holes, running scared for safe hiding somewhere in the back swamps.

Lauren had suggested they use the old wagon path as a short cut towards the sloping banks of the Village River. She was talking about how the boat loggers had cleared the land of its oak, cypress and tupelo, the business that had brought money into Blackwater.

Under the silvery moonlight, Jack had stopped for a few minutes to take a look around the abandoned extraction sheds. He was considering the lie of the land; its proximity to the abandoned Whistler settlement and his sorrel.

'Have you seen something?' Lauren asked.

'Can't see much, but I think it was a coyote, a fox, maybe. Something must have got it startled back a ways. I'm a tad worried about *what*.'

'Maybe the swamper girl sent out her Bigfoot buddy to keep an eye on you.'

'Half of that could be right,' Jack muttered slow and thoughtful. 'What's the syrupy smell?'

'Decaying stuff. Pine resins and the like. This area's saturated with it. It's not what I had in mind, Jack.'

'Nor me. But maybe it's just as well. I think we're being trailed.'

'Why would anyone be trailing *us*?'

'Not us. *Me*. And there is a reason.'

Despite Lauren Kyle's obvious attractions, to Jack she was a bit of a triviality. He'd quickly realized there was nothing for him, very little to hold his interest. Even so, he didn't want to put her in any danger.

He stared hard across and along the reed banks of the still waters, closed his eyes for a second or two, listening. The night insects had stopped their nearby clamour, and all Jack's senses told him there was a nearby danger.

'Jack, what are you doing?' she protested when Jack turned and drew her down from the buckboard.

'For God's sake, I'm not going to hurt you,' Jack hissed, jostling her behind the bulk of a rusted piece of machinery. 'There's someone out there who might, though. Just stay down and don't make a sound. You'll be safe enough, and I'll be right here.'

Lauren was going to say more but changed her mind when she saw Jack was suddenly holding his Colt. Her jaw tightened and she lowered her shoulders, shrinking into the protection of the iron stump grinder.

'If any harm comes to me this night, I'll be holding you responsible,' she seethed.

Jack offered a rapid grin to the absurdity. 'You were after this jaunt more than me,' he replied quietly, adding, 'our tryst ends here, I take it,' slightly louder, as he veered away. Crouching low in the gleaming grass, he wondered if the sway of the moss on the tupelos was from a night breeze, or if someone was getting close, almost upon them.

He kneeled beside the trestle of a dirt and ivy-filled sluice, waited for whoever it was to emerge through the darkness. He was calm enough. His years of high-stake gambling in treacherous company afforded him that. But a minute later, he cursed silently at the pallid face of Loop Ducet, staring out from the waterside bull thistles.

Ducet wasn't who Jack was expecting. He figured on Harry Grice, the man he'd shot and shamed in the High Chair Saloon. It wasn't the sort of argument a hired gun forgot too readily. Ducet was casting a look this way and that, back towards the horse and buggy. Then he turned away and Jack realized there was someone with him.

Lauren moved and Jack gave more silent curses. He'd hoped she'd have the sense to stay put, and cursed again. Melba Savoy would know how to handle the situation. The spooky bayou was her territory, her playground. She might not have the culture, but right now she'd make a fine partner, Jack was thinking.

He peered around the rotting wood supports at what he thought was movement. He could see Ducet, who was still crouching, but to one side there was now another shadowy silhouette, then two together emerging silently behind them.

They were moving closer now and Jack involuntarily sniffed the air. The liveryman in Blackwater had told him that genuine swamp people were odorous from a double stone's throw away. *That counts for Ducet*, Jack decided. *So, who the hell are the other three?*

'Where is the sumbitch? How'd you know he's here?'

'He's here … probably watchin' us right now.'

'This place looks like one o' them Bible towns – a place o' pestilence.'

'Yeah. I heard there's wild bears sleepin' in the old cabins.'

'Shut it for Chris'sakes, you two. If *I* can hear you, *he* can,' said a stifled voice.

Silently, Jack eased back the hammer of his Colt. The four men were new positioning themselves behind the collapsed timbers of a logged cabin. The ruin was matted with buckthorn, and Jack was only aware of movement, no real shapes or faces.

After a short while, Jack heard what sounded like

arguments in hushed undertones. He heard his name. Someone coughed nervously, and he wondered what it was they wanted with him, if they were out for a kill.

A strained voice that Jack nearly recognized shouted out. 'Rogan, I know you're there. Show yourself, feller. We've been sent to talk to you.'

Yeah? By who? Jack wondered. 'Then get on with it,' he shouted back. 'I can hear you.'

The whispering continued and then, without warning, one of them grunted and rushed headlong. He was a gaunt young man with long white hair, who now was very plainly geared up for a killing. He was hefting a sawed-off shotgun, yelling like a Rebel at Cemetery Ridge. And Jack had seen him before.

'I seem to remember tellin' you I was through with second chances,' he seethed angrily and triggered his Colt at the figure running towards him.

There was brief flash of gunfire, then through the mix of cordite and ground mist rose a gasping cry. The assailant was going down, ploughing into the dark grass as though its body had lost all support.

Jack could see a dark, glistening spread of blood high on the man's chest where his bullet had struck. 'Goddamn albino didn't even get off a shot,' he rasped. 'At least you won't be taking a switch to any more poor dogs.'

At the outbreak of shooting, Lauren Kyle's horse

went careering off into the darkness with the buck-board bouncing wildly behind it.

'The rig's gone, Lauren. Just stay where you are. Whoever it is can't get to you,' he called out, hoping he was right.

Immediately, a wild volley broke across the bayou land, bullets hammering into the base of the trestle Jack was hiding behind. Chunks of decayed wood showered around him as he hunkered down. *Goddamnit, who the hell are they*? he cursed. There was one question answered, though: they did want him dead. He cursed again. 'Is this the sort of talk you had in mind? Got worried I'd answer back?' he yelled mockingly.

Through the resulting noise and menacing whine of bullets, Jack sensed his assailants were spreading to his left and right. They were attempting to outflank him, and he had to move.

He dropped his shoulder and quickly rolled away from shelter. He travelled six or seven feet and rose to one knee. Through the thin hang of mist and gun-smoke, he made out two figures looking almost directly at him, one of much bigger build than the other.

Without cover now, Jack brought up his Colt. There was no time for trading abuse, considering a way out. He had to bring them down. Fully extending his right arm, he pointed the barrel and fired belly high at the leading gunman.

The man stopped in his tracks and Jack fired again. The man stumbled forward a short pace, firing his Colt into the ground before his legs gave way. He coughed, fell flat on his face and gagged silent and final.

Jack only recognized Loop Ducet when he saw the bandolier of rope around the man's shoulder. 'What the hell's going on here?' he muttered.

He threw himself down as more bullets sliced and whipped through the longer grass. Then he took a breath and sat up, both hands clasped tight around the Colt. But he didn't fire. The larger man had turned towards the ghostly cypresses curtaining the waterside.

In the silence that followed, Jack picked up on other sounds drifting in from beyond where Laura was hiding. *They're coming from town,* he thought. *Who the hell's side are they going to be on?*

'Get back, I'll give you cover,' someone shouted from the trees.

'I've just tried, goddamnit. You go out there,' came the reply.

'We'll soon have half o' Blackwater down on us. Blast him out.'

Jack cursed because he didn't quite recognize the voice of Harry Grice. Calculating the odds, he waited for a lull in the shooting then he leapt to his feet and ran. Avoiding the immediate hammer of guns, he headed towards the dark hulk of a dredger bucket. He stretched out his left hand, swung to one side and got thumped hard in the middle of his back. It felt like he'd been hit by a door as he plunged gasping into the sheltering curve of the huge container. He cursed aloud, doubled up as bullets crashed into the iron above him.

He rolled onto his side, lay his Colt down and reached his hand behind him. He probed cautiously with his fingers but felt no blood. The passing bullet had hurt, but effected little more than tearing his jacket and punching air from his lungs.

'Help's on the way, Lauren. I can here 'em,' he shouted. 'Keep your head down.'

Jack hoped his words would carry, maybe send the guns packing. *Give the dog another goddam day*, he thought.

And there was silence from then on. Jack got to his feet and levelled his Colt. He listened, but there were no sounds other than those he'd heard earlier from the direction of town.

'Lauren, I'm covering you until the cavalry arrive. It sounds like they're headed your way. Just hang on,' he continued.

When the first eager towner rode into Lis Etang, it was all over. Blanco Bilis and Loop Ducet were dead and two more were gone.

Lauren Kyle was silent with suppressed terror as she

was led to safety by a couple of townsfolk.

'I'll wager that's the end of our courtship,' Jack muttered, replacing the cylinder in his Colt. His calm exterior hid frustration and anger, and he was feeling like hell.

12

Sheriff Milo Buckmaster stood in the doorway of McAllister's carpenter and coffin maker shop. He was staring disappointedly at the canvas-covered figures.

He was a straightforward town lawman who usually did what was expected of him, usually by decree of those who pulled the Blackwater strings. Occasionally, there was an outbreak of violence, and every now and again there might be some gunplay, like when Jack Rogan and Harry Grice had their difference of opinion in the High Chair Saloon.

'Did you know these men?' he asked.

'Knowin's a bit strong,' McAllister answered.

'Neither of 'em's a great loss,' Buckmaster rumbled.

The carpenter looked up from his workbench for a moment. 'It can only be to your advantage, Buck. Believe me,' he said, then continued sawing planked wood.

'I guess so,' Buckmaster continued. With that, he

lifted the covers, took a second, confirming look at the bodies. 'Make boxes. Coffins are too good,' he offered drily, and grimaced.

Out on the boardwalk he met the mayor and Morton Pegg. Both men were dour-faced and tense-looking. They started right in, demanding to know what steps he proposed taking against Jack Rogan.

'Didn't have too much trouble before he arrived, Buck,' Hockton Marney said. 'Nothing that we couldn't take care of between us. It's all got out of order.'

'Yeah,' Pegg agreed. 'Slap-hand fighting in the street on a Friday night's one thing. Murder's another.'

Buckmaster sniffed assertively. 'For whatever reason, it was four men goin' out to the old stump workin's who wanted to commit murder,' he stated. 'Now, two o' them's been killed and two's escaped. That's what Jack Rogan an' Lauren Kyle says happened, an' there's much circumstantial evidence to support it. I got no plans to do anythin' more.'

'None of us took that Rogan for a hired gun, Sheriff,' Pegg asserted.

'I don't reckon he is. But I know he's a fast thinker. A quality them two losers could've done with,' Buckmaster retorted.

McAllister was now nailing planks, but he hadn't missed a word of what was going on outside his workshop.

The sheriff was right and held the cards, for once was surprisingly determined. Pegg and Marney hurled angry insinuations, but were forced to give up and stomped off angrily towards the High Chair Saloon.

As though he'd been waiting for Marney and Pegg to leave, Gaston Savoy was next to enter McAllister's workshop. The previous night he'd been concerned when Melba told him Jack Rogan had ridden from town. But later, not wanting to get involved or show his hand, he'd stayed behind. He'd waited anxiously, was one of the first to see the corpses when they were brought in after the ruckus. Now, after some troubled overnight thinking, he was responding to the sheriff's request for a meeting.

'Come up yet with a reason why Loop Ducet would want to go after Jack Rogan?' Buckmaster asked.

'Nothin' more'n what I said last night,' Savoy replied with some degree of truth. 'Loop was a mean wretch. He was never goin' to end up on a sick bed.'

'He was a friend of Homer Lamb's,' Buckmaster stated.

'What's that supposed to mean?' Savoy bridled.

'I'm lookin' for two fellers who got away, Mr Savoy. Rogan says one of 'em was wide, maybe big-bearded.'

'That could fit more'n a dozen men from in an' around Blackwater.'

'Yeah, but they wouldn't be friends of Ducet's, would

they? I don't suppose he got his name, or carried that goddamn catch rope for nothin'.'

'Are you sayin' Homer was involved in that trouble, Sheriff?'

Buckmaster shook his head. 'Not necessarily. I'm just followin' up on what I've been told. I've talked to the man himself, but he claims to know nothin'.' The sheriff paused to study Savoy a moment. 'He can't prove he wasn't out there, last night, an' I can't prove he was,' he added.

'So you've got nothin'.'

'Yeah, deadlock. Even though every man an' his dog knows that Lamb's goin' to call it with Jack Rogan.'

'I know what's comin' down here, Sheriff,' Savoy rasped. 'I've been runnin' up against this sort o' prejudice for a good ten years. An' none more so than this mornin' here in town. Just because one o' my flock happened to be shootin' his mouth an' gun off, don't mean a damn thing. Maybe Loop's explosive nature got the better of him. Maybe it was a personal thing. Maybe he's suddenly fallen in with even badder local company.'

'That's a lot o' maybes, Mr Savoy. Morton Pegg an' the mayor's been tryin' to railroad me into bringin' charges against Rogan.'

'And?'

'I told 'em, no deal.'

'Huh. What wouldn't Morton Pegg give to see us all brought down, eh, Sheriff? A chance to move on new land for his sawmills – to open up his wretched business once again. The mayor's got other reasons for wantin' to see the back o' me.'

'Well, the facts say all Rogan's done is defend himself and Miss Lauren. Do you know how they're set this mornin'?'

'There's no sign o' the lady. Rogan's got a backache an' one or two things on his mind. I'm thinkin' of ridin' out to Whistler with him till he cools off. It's a lot safer out on the bayou.'

'Yeah? Tell that to the night crackers of Lis Etang. I heard you're holdin' Rogan against his will … that you've got somethin' belongs to him.'

'Hah. Does he sound like the kind of feller who'd go along with that? Are we talkin' o' the same person?'

'Well that's the buzz. I've got to ask.'

'An' you did, Sheriff.' With a curt nod in the direction of McAllister, Savoy turned on his heel and strode away.

McAllister immediately looked to Buckmaster. 'The whole thing's kind o' curious, don't you think?'

Buckmaster was still pondering on Savoy's response about Jack Rogan. 'What is? What's curious?' he asked.

'We get ourselves a peaceful society goin', then them swampers move in, an' gunfights break out all over.'

'You offerin' a connection?' Buckmaster asked.

'Connection, coincidence, it's all the same kidney. Can't pretend it ain't.'

'You're gettin' to sound like one o' them rednecks Savoy's been harpin' on about. Gettin' a tad picky about the bloodline of a neighbour.'

'Picky?' McAllister exclaimed. 'Why there's town kids wonderin' where their cats an' dogs are disappearin' to. You understand what I'm saying, Sheriff? You think that's daybreak mist hangin' over their goddamn tents? You ever smelled hillbilly stew?'

Buckmaster shook his head tolerantly. 'Got anythin' else on your mind, Mac?'

'Yeah. Me an' one or two others have been wonderin' who this Jack Rogan feller might be. You know, what's he here for? Has Savoy brought him in on purpose, like ... backup if he needs to win arguments? Folk don't take kindly to them sort o' manners, Sheriff.'

'You know what I think, Mac?'

'What?'

'I think the minute I've left here, you'll be back to chewin' on mescal beans.'

McAllister snorted, and set about assembling the two plain coffins. 'Was only tryin' to be helpful,' he muttered. 'These men ain't here to cut a rug. There's somethin' in the wind, I know it.'

The carpenter wasn't such a sharp blade any more.

Nowadays, he was indulged as a harmless prophet of doom. But this time, Buckmaster had a gut feeling that something bad was about to happen.

Jack heard the sound of his own footfall in the quiet that descended when he walked into the High Chair Saloon. It was midday, and there was a good crowd of drinkers at the long bar. The poker and blackjack layouts hadn't opened up yet, and only the tiger on the faro box was turning.

To a man, they watched him, pretending not to. Eyes were raised to the back-bar mirror, before quickly dropping away. Yesterday, Jack had been the outsider from Whistler who rode a ploughboy mule; today he was a killer of men.

He walked to a vacant spot that emerged at the bar, and ordered whiskey. The man at the pianola sat immobile, his fingers suspended over the black and white keys. As Jack's drink clicked hard on the counter, the man hit a key, and the roll started up with a lively, kicking-heel tune.

The barkeep nodded and Jack nodded back. At a table near the door, he pulled up a chair. There was a deck of cards and he started organizing them into suits and numbers. His hands were steady but he looked pale.

Five minutes later, the batwings swung aside and

Gaston Savoy came in. He saw Jack and made straight for his table.

'I was wondering where you'd be. Take a seat,' Jack said without looking up. 'I want you to return my horse and thousand dollars, now. I want the hell out of this town,' he added trying to avoid anyone overhearing.

Savoy took a moment to consider Jack's words. 'It shouldn't have happened,' he offered. 'What the hell Loop was doin' out there, I don't know. Really, I don't. What I do know is I can't let a little misunderstandin' mess up our association. My plans ain't bore fruit yet.'

Jack continued to shuffle the cards. He knew Savoy wanted to keep him around for whatever reason, and last night was almost certainly a lead up to more trouble. To a professional card player, the shooting dead of two men wasn't an everyday occurrence. He knew he was being pushed into a worsening situation.

'I hear there's some disturbance back at Whistler. There's some still there, an' some have gone back. Ride out with me an' you can see how the sorrel's doin. It'll give us time to consider one or two things.' Savoy gave Jack a hard, black-eyed stare as he got to his feet. 'Half an hour,' he said.

Jack dealt himself a hand, turned the cards over and considered the result. 'Total rubbish,' he muttered. 'Just as well I'm leaving.' He carefully replaced the cards on the bottom of the deck, drained his glass and stood up. He wanted to be gone now, away from Whistler, Frog Hollow, Lis Etang, goddamn Blackwater and anyone remotely connected with them.

At the batwings, he held the doors apart for a moment. He turned his head to look at the groups of shapes and faces that were still watching him. Then he walked away, trying to recall the voice he'd heard out on the bayou. He knew it … just couldn't tag on a name or face. *Half an hour, it is*, he thought. *And I've considered one or two things of my own.*

13

Jack was sitting out on the double-planked levee of Gaston Savoy's cabin. He was watching the wood ducks that lapped up weed from under the fishing platforms. At that moment, Beaumont, Texas seemed further away than it had ever been. He didn't feel much like someone who had made a sizeable grubstake, collected a handful of prized, personal possessions and was returning home to consider investing in a future. He had those things going for him, all right, but for the time being they had been taken away, sort of confiscated, and he wanted them back. For the umpteenth time he checked that his Colt held a fully loaded cylinder.

Whistler's settlement had been created around a clutch of crudely built cabins. On the far side of the broad compound, one or two homesick family members were exchanging concerns with malingerers. They were packing chattels, still preparing for their belated journey to Blackwater. The small group weren't quite so enthusiastic to make a move as they had been. They'd just got used to Savoy and his henchmen not being around to dominate them.

Melba had been right, Jack mused. This was her father's dream, a dream that was fast becoming a delusion. *And you took all my worldly goods,* he thought. *You deserve all you're going to get.*

Over in the pole corral, the sorrel had its nose buried deep in an oat sack. The horse was still under guard, but Jack guessed that if he wandered too close, the man would make a run for it. The new found reputation of Jack Rogan had travelled ahead. In a couple of local incidents, Jack had gone a lot further than dishing out a few slaps and punches.

It was a standing that suited Jack. It gave him the moments he needed to consider a strategy, possible line of attack.

A door of one of the larger cabins opened and Homer Lamb appeared. Jack watched the wide-shouldered man with the long beard take a long searching look his way. He didn't know, only half suspected it had been Lamb down at Lis Etang, who tried to put him in the canning factory. Then again, like Savoy's thinking, with the hullabaloo and darkness, it could easily have been someone else.

Minutes later, Melba emerged from the settlement's old forage store and started across the compound.

Lamb spoke to her, but she ignored him, kept walking in Jack's direction. She hadn't spoken to him since the gunfight, but he didn't think he'd improved his reputation in her determined eyes.

'Good morning, Melba. I guess you know what I'm doing back here, what about you?' he asked coolly.

Melba didn't answer back. She just studied him, her shoulders dropping casually.

Yeah, take a lot to unnerve you, Jack thought. *Some other time, certainly another place and who knows....*

'I lived here for ten years,' she replied. 'Coming back to say goodbye's not so strange.'

'No,' he agreed. 'My ma told me that everyone who says goodbye isn't gone.'

'She'll be expecting you back then?'

'Oh yeah. But we've been through that, Melba.'

'You still thinking about what happened out at Lis Etang?'

'I know *what* happened. I'm thinking about who was behind it – the two who got away.'

'How about *why*?'

'Well, they weren't out there fishing, that's for sure. It must have something to do with me asking questions about Winge Tedder. It was that soon after.'

Melba showed surprise. 'If it did have anything to do with it, I'm sorry.'

'Okay, but it won't alter anything. Now, either your

clan's come to town, or a local rancher's lost some of his herd.'

Gaston Savoy was walking towards them. He was flanked by his sons Eliot and John, nephew Cletus and a family mix of Lambs and Boudros.

'They've come en masse this time. It's likely one of them knows something.'

'They've probably been off chasin' coons. It's something you can't do from Blackwater,' Melba replied.

Savoy looked their way and nodded an acknowledgment. He held up his hand in a way that meant he wasn't going to trouble Jack with anything just yet.

Jack stood and put on his hat. 'Melba, about this man, this agency that's buying you out?' he inquired.

'What about it?'

'I know your pa's had some pretty big offers to sell up over the years, particularly from Morton Pegg. I'm wondering why he turned them down but accepted this particular one. Have you any idea?'

'No. But I know Pa wouldn't ever sell out if he thought there'd be loggers moving in. Not after what the Pegg lumber company has done to the land. He doesn't sound or look much like it, but in his own way he respects the country as much as any of us.'

'In his own way while you lived there, that's for sure,' Jack agreed quietly, slightly questioning. 'These people's credentials are genuine … blue-chip, I suppose.'

'I know he's a government man. Something to do with the Department of the Interior. He says he'll fix things up real good here. It'll stop the loggers moving in.'

'Yeah, government men always mean well when it comes to land issues,' Jack started. 'The Sioux and Cheyenne will tell you as much.'

'Times are changing,' Melba said flatly.

'Yeah, *times* have. There's still a lot of *folk* who haven't, though, Melba. Do you happen to know what sort of money's involved?'

'It's obviously enough to get all our people resettled. And then some to give us a good chance – a stake.'

'Hmm. Whatever it was, it's probably worth ten times that,' Jack suggested. He turned slowly, letting his eyes rove across the lush, thickly timbered setting. *And if you did happen to be a lumberman, a hundred times that*, he thought.

When somebody called out for Melba, Jack ambled across to the corral. Kept separate from the mules, the sorrel immediately stomped, tossed its head with pleasure. Jack laughed, nosed it happily under the nervous eyes of two young, but well-armed stock guards.

'Keep calm, fellers. I've done my quota killings for this week,' he said wryly. He patted the sorrel's silken muzzle, pushed his face in close to the side of its head, the blind side of the guards. 'Don't go all green-eyed when you see me ride out on one of their knob-heads. I'll see you later. We've got unfinished business.'

A short while later, Jack rode from the settlement. He was free to come and go more or less as he wished. Nobody was going to challenge him while Savoy held his money and his sorrel remained under house arrest. But even if he had his horse under him, it was unlikely he would have made a run for it. What interested him today was finding out what had happened to Winge Tedder.

Jack had heard that Tedder was suspected of being on Morton Pegg's payroll, that Pegg's crony, Harry Grice had been seen with Tedder soon before he disappeared. From the way people spoke of him, Tedder didn't sound like a hardcase or a weakling, but it looked pretty certain now that something bad had happened to him. There was other stuff on Jack's mind that didn't dovetail, like Pegg's connection with Tedder and the offer made for the land around Whistler.

Jack took a deep, troubled breath, let Savoy's saddle mule carry him at a shuffling trot away from the settlement towards Lis Etang.

'What in tarnation's wrong with you, Hockton?' Beatrice Marney said. 'You've been like a mare full of cockleburs all morning. What do you want the surrey for? You look like hell.'

The mayor looked miserable because he felt it. One of the reasons being that his wife was spending most of her time with Gaston Savoy.

'If you spent more time at home, I wouldn't look such a dupe when you're painting the town with that bull-necked piker, Savoy.'

'Ah, it is about *you*, then. I thought as much. For what it's worth, I've allowed Gaston to take me *some* places because you're always too busy to take me *any-where*. And the fact he's been holding a torch for me for ten years, isn't easy to ignore. I'm not totally without compassion.'

'Hah, you could've fooled me.'

'What does that mean?' Beatrice said, but without emotion. That feeling was long gone. Her husband had always wanted everything of value he could lay his hands on. Such was his avarice that it sometimes included goods of little or no value. Unfortunately Beatrice had been one of the packages, but she hadn't realized until it was too late.

'It means I'm late for an important meeting,' Marney barked, and hurried off without another word.

A half hour later, Marney was pulling up at the back office of the Morton Pegg Lumber Company, where a bunch of men quietly waited.

Marney's face set even further into grief when he saw Harry Grice playing solitaire on top of an empty telegraph bench. Morton Pegg's gunhand had been held in low regard by the mayor since the fiasco at Lis Etang. Jack Rogan had emerged only shaken from that incident, and therefore it probably seemed like a triumph for Gaston Savoy. It was a reason why the mayor wanted the sale of Whistler to be completed as soon as possible.

Marney was also surprised to see Homer Lamb at the office.

'Well he's got to be somewhere, but he wants somethin' done about Rogan,' Grice explained. 'He reckons that Rogan still half suspects he was out there. He's worried the son-of-a-bitch will come up with somethin'. Ain't that so, Homer?'

'He made out lucky in the dark an' all,' Lamb growled. 'It won't happen next time.'

'I wouldn't have thought you wanted a next time,' Marney said. 'At the moment we're only interested in tying up the deal. Before Savoy changes his mind.'

'He ain't goin' to do that,' Lamb argued. 'I know him better'n any of you. He's committed himself ... needs one hell of a pile o' dollars to see it through.'

'Yes, *our* pile, *our* investment,' Marney said, a touch irritably. 'And that includes Bunce's money from the Railroad holdings. We had to give a king's ransom and a trumped-up story to persuade Savoy to sell out. Chester's probably riding out right now to get that part sorted. Let's get this over and done with.'

Marney and Pegg drove their own rigs, with an outrider each. Pegg lit up one of his Coronas, made the journey pass thinking about his profit from an incalculable quantity of new timber. Marney sat on the edge of his seat, staring dully at the passing landscape. He felt like a music hall juggler on stage in a wild cow town. He had too many balls in the air, was very concerned about audience response if he stumbled and dropped them.

14

A mile out of town, Jack ground-hitched his mule. 'Wait here,' he said quietly. 'It's a lot better than going back or going forward.'

He went on, walking carefully between dark holes from where old cypress and tupelo stumps had been dragged or blasted from the swampy ground. The trees had gone to sawmills at Port Neche and Pegg's Mill or straight to the turpentine plant at De Quirrel.

There had been no rain since Jack had ridden through the spooky bayou to Frog Hollow in pursuit of Cletus Savoy. Old tracks from footfalls and hoof marks had dried some, but were still visible. Getting closer to Lis Etang, he didn't notice the water rats until they scurried up and off a coiled cypress root into the thickly reeded water.

Warily, he edged closer to the edge of the bayou creek, cursing under his breath when he made out the shape of a partly submerged range hat. He knew instinctively he was near to where Winge Tedder had died; the other side of the clearing from where he'd fought off the darkness attackers.

The big water rats were already closing in for another nose around. Jack couldn't imagine where or what they'd been doing. 'No one's going to last long down in there,' he murmured.

He turned away from the grim sight, looking up to see the top courses of a brick chimney, beyond the low vegetation. It was the empty steam-cutter house, and he pushed through the eel grass for a closer look. It was where trees used to be sliced for boating to Port Neche, and at one end of a long tumbledown building, he saw three rigs and a few tethered horses. One of the rigs was Pegg's stylish trap; another was Hockton Marney's surrey. *Not exactly mayor country. What's he doing with Pegg? And who the hell else is here?* were among his first thoughts. He guessed he wasn't too far from finding out, maybe from getting an answer to some of the questions he had. A curious, visceral feeling told him he'd discover what part Gaston Savoy would have him play in all of it.

Standing alone, Harry Grice had his own reasons for keeping a slightly nervous eye on his surroundings. But he wasn't suspicious of the lily pads that floated close. There was always something littering the surface of the bayous, stuff fallen from the cypresses or broken loose of the banksides.

The vegetation swirled slowly, drifted on past the works buildings. Jack strode as fast as he could from the water, shuddering with disgust, hauling himself out through the reeds over the muddy bank. He swiped wet vegetation from his face, making sure he hadn't been seen. He hoped his Colt still worked, pondered on the risk of it misfiring.

Scrubby cover dotted the distance between creek and buildings and he made use of what there was in a series of quick, stealthy dashes.

Reaching a building, he pressed up alongside a broken-framed window, sliding close enough to hear the clear drift of voices. It didn't look or sound like it was the first time the place had been used as a clandestine meeting place, and it didn't take long for him to establish that four men were inside. Morton Pegg, Hockton Marney, and two others named Chester and Bunce. Both these names were familiar to him. Chester was the purported government agent with funds to purchase Whistler and its hinterland. Benedict Bunce was an executive of the Gulf Railroad Company.

The get-together was expressive and noisy. Pegg, Marney and Bunce were pressing Chester to force closure on the deal with Gaston Savoy. Chester protested that Savoy might spook and get suspicious.

'We've got to get it signed an' sealed, goddamnit,'

said the voice, which Jack now recognized as Benedict Bunce's. 'Every hour we delay, the greater risk o' the truth gettin' out. If that redneck somehow hits on our branch line through the middle o' Whistler we're finished. We've all sunk too much into this venture to have it not happen.'

Now the land surrounding Lis Etang had been stripped bare, the only cost-effective way for Morton Pegg and his investors to get their hands on a new timber supply was by hauling into the empty Whistler township and onto the railroad's flat-bed wagons. There was no other way of hauling big timber further north.

'Yeah, you've got to hasten things up, Chester,' Pegg added. 'For what it's worth, I don't think you'll be warning him off. He's got other interests to sidetrack him in Blackwater besides his people.'

There were then a few moments of awkward, telling silence. Before listening to Marney's reaction to Pegg's insinuation, Jack had heard enough. He'd come to Lis Etang thinking there'd be answers and he'd found them. And he'd wager that the murder of Winge Tedder and the attack on him were tangled up in the deal.

He was considering retracing his route back to the creek when a man armed with a rifle appeared at the corner of the building. Before he turned to look in

Jack's direction, Jack had backed quickly into the taller grass. But you could see where he'd been standing, listening.

The man gave a warning yell. He'd seen the dark stain beneath the window where creek water had dripped, pooling thin on a broken flagstone.

Jack waited until Grice had responded to the outcry, then he ran fast back the way he'd come, but this time along the bank.

A door opened as Jack rushed to the tethered horses. Harry Grice let out a holler as the horses lunged away, and Jack threw himself at the neck of a sturdy buckskin. A gun roared and bullets thumped close. Jack swung into the saddle, kicking his heels and shouting for the horse to run.

Within seconds, riders were racing to try to cut him off, hoping they knew the treacherous ground better than Jack did. One man he sighted was an employee of Morton Pegg, but another was Homer Lamb.

'So that's who the horses were waiting for,' he muttered. 'And I should have recognized your voice, you son-of-a-bitch.'

If his cartridge charges were damp from his wading in the creek water, Jack knew he'd be in big trouble as he swung his Colt around and fired a defensive shot at Lamb. But the shot was too hasty and it was the horse that buckled, the rider falling, then rolling clear.

Jack cursed and heeled his mount forward. But now the Pegg gunman was quickly gaining on him, and he cursed again. 'Run,' he shouted. 'Go join the herd. It must be a goddamn liberty day somewhere.'

Jack wasn't far off the wagon road between Blackwater and Lis Etang, more than halfway to Whistler. 'There's one coming to take your place,' he thought, watching the horse raise its head and sniff before running off. He settled behind the stump of an old uprooted tupelo, drew his Colt and rested the barrel on his left arm.

The rider appeared on cue, didn't have time to sense the lurking danger before he was hit.

There was no slip-up from Jack this time and taking careful aim he fired twice. 'No more paydays for you, feller. Let's hope Pegg honours your kin,' he rasped quietly. He ran straight to the man's horse without taking another look at the rider, scooped the reins and swung into the saddle.

After running the horse for ten minutes Jack knew he'd make it to Whistler. The chasing riders were still in pursuit and they weren't going to ride off, but he had just enough of an advantage.

Jack barely made it to the safety of the outlying Whistler shacks and cabins when Harry Grice brought his men racing through the trees, raising their firearms and firing indiscriminately.

Jack knew the men were now acting on orders. They were to clear the settlement, leave nothing behind – make the area safe for their paymasters to begin their voracious schemes. The profits from the vast tracts of timber were so great they would worry about the consequences later.

The once peaceful and still bayous were now suddenly riven by the sounds of gunfire. Jack sensed he'd really got himself between a rock and a hard place.

15

Gaston Savoy showed a haggard face when he looked up from his wounded son, Eliot. 'You brought the hounds of hell back with you,' he accused.

'Believe me, Savoy, they were coming for you one way or another,' Jack replied sharply. 'I had some things wrong … not all of it. I'll be taking what's mine and heading away from this stricken place. If I don't return, you and yours are old enough, certainly ugly enough, to sort yourselves out. Remember, none of this is my doing.'

'You remember, I still got those thousand dollars,' Savoy said. 'If you want to know what snake pit it's hidden in, you'll be back. Besides, you'll never make it anywhere now.'

'On the sorrel I will,' Jack insisted, flinching as a speculative rifle bullet smashed through a side window. 'Not that there's a choice. This old place of yours might keep outsiders out, but it also keeps insiders in.'

'How the hell do they figure they can get away with it?' Savoy raged.

'Most likely the same reason they had before they made a deal with *you*,' Jack snapped back. 'But things have changed. Of a sudden they're desperate … figure they're going to lose everything they've been dreaming of,' Jack continued. 'They'll probably say you were reneging on their lawful acquisition of the land. If they testify you attacked them here, who'll be around to say otherwise? You'll all be with Winge Tedder, sleeping underwater.'

Jack eased back the cabin door on its heavy hinges, looked across the empty, flattened grass of the settlement's compound. 'If I do make it back to town, with any luck there'll be a posse here about nine o'clock. With or without me. Knowing every goddamn rat and snake hole like you do, take advantage of them. Even with a couple of slingshots you should be able to hold out till then.'

Jack was considering his move across to the corral, when Melba suddenly pushed through the narrow back door.

Jack turned. 'What's this? A charm?' he said, not unkindly.

'Sort of,' Melba replied quietly. 'It's made from coney bones. I've used it to bring me all sorts of luck. Try it out.'

'Thank you, I will. You folk are something else,' Jack said with a smile and a shake of his head as he left the cabin.

In the failing light he had no trouble getting to the corral. 'It's a long story,' he told the single guard. 'But if I was you, I'd find somewhere safe and keep my head down for the next couple of hours. It's the only way you're going to stay alive,' he added brusquely.

Jack saddled his big mare, gave reassuring words. It seemed much darker within the closeness of the tupelos and cypress, their ghostly tendrils of Spanish moss. Waiting for full dark, he hoped the attackers would think twice before moving through such an eerie and treacherous place.

'It's a poor set of legs that'll stand around to get hurt. Let's show the sons-of-bitches how to run,' he said with a new confidence.

In the main street of Blackwater Jack stood rubbing the sorrel's forehead, feeding it a plug of sugar cane. There were raised voices and much confusion. Angry men mounted up and checked their handguns, waiting for Sheriff Buckmaster to lead them out.

'Never thought we'd be ridin' to help them swampers,' one of them shouted.

'You're not,' returned another. 'You're helpin' fellow citizens.'

Jack was both impressed and bewildered. He had been afraid the townsfolk would refuse to rally to the aid of the bayou clans, despite the fact most of them were now virtually neighbours. Jack thought their willingness to create a posse had something to do with their futures being controlled by one or two opportunists. Of those Whistler men who'd recently moved to town, most were eager to take a gun to simply help family and friends. Watching them get together, Jack felt a hollow kind of relief. He was hopeful they'd get there in time to deal with Pegg and Grice; before hired guns caused more harm.

'We've done our bit,' he muttered to the sorrel. 'I've done just about everything man or beast could. I've been robbed, shot at, wounded and chased through wildernesses that are infested with all kinds of poisonous critters. And from a bunch of throwbacks who held *you* hostage while I was unarmed and hog-tied. Goddamnit, now I'm back here getting *them* help.'

Getting his horse and then his money back would go some way to Jack overlooking the treatment meted out by Gaston Savoy. 'I never was much on leaving a game without *some* profit,' he said. 'So let's go and get those dollars back.'

Jack heeled the big sorrel into an easy, powerful lope, taking them past the High Chair Saloon and out of town, back towards the wagon road. He was heading off to the west, in the direction of Whistler when he noticed the dark sky above the tops of the heavy stands of timber. 'That's smoke, not cloud,' he muttered. 'But there's nothing to burn like that out here,' he added, pulling the sorrel to a halt. 'Except the goddamn cabins. Those sons-of-bitches want the bayou trees so bad, they'll burn 'em down in desperation.' Then he caught the first whiff of smoke carried by the night breeze, and his blood chilled.

There were still some youngsters out at Whistler. For one reason or another, they and their families hadn't yet removed to Blackwater. And they weren't the only ones. Jack raised his hand to his shirt pocket, felt the bone ornament given to him by Melba. 'You can't ignore 'em,' he said thoughtfully. 'So, let's go and help 'em.'

The attackers had first overrun the two empty Boudro cabins on the eastern perimeter of the compound. Harry Grice and his gunmen stormed from one cabin to the next, lashing out at anything that caught their eye. But Hockton Marney stayed behind. Among the remains of what had been abandoned he'd spotted a jar of moonshine standing beside a pot-belly stove. He gasped uneasily, felt he'd never needed a drink more in his life.

What was happening now at the old Whistler

settlement wasn't Marney's style – not this close-up stuff where you got dirty, did your own killing. The mayor was a back-room schemer, always had been. He had wanted to pull out when Chester and Bunce had refused to chase after Jack Rogan. But Morton Pegg had forced him to join them. Now the lumber merchant was arguing they had the chance to wipe out the entire Whistler contingent. 'It'll look like a bitter family rivalry got the better of 'em,' he'd suggested. 'It's nothin' your regular, God-fearin' townsfolk won't accept.'

Realizing Pegg's mind had gone beyond reason, Marney wanted out. His nerves were shredded and he was trembling with fear. 'Maybe a slug of this stuff,' he said. 'Just something for the nerves.'

As both his hands closed around the neck of the jar, a window exploded with a crash. A bullet smashed low into his belly, another into his chest. He fell against the stove, gasping with misery, his eyes closing as the liquor fell from his clutching fingers.

'They never said anythin' about burnin',' Homer Lamb seethed as he ran stumbling towards the settlement. With one hand he gripped his Walker Colt, with the other he brushed aside tendrils of trailing moss and peered at the scene ahead. He shook his head in ignorance, couldn't figure just how he'd come to find himself in this position. He was fighting his own people, watching his old home go up in flames. He vaguely knew it had started with his resentment of Gaston Savoy, an irrational need to overthrow the old guard. But it had got out of hand when Jack Rogan arrived. Now it looked like the only way out was by aligning himself with Harry Grice and a corrupt business scheme.

He approached Pegg and Grice, who were holed up in the cookshack. 'It's just not goin' to get us what we want. There's got to be some other way,' he said, his voice near to desperation. 'If anyone gets wind of what's happenin' ... starts puttin' two an' two together, they'll send for US marshals.'

'That's just what we need,' Pegg sneered back. 'Someone who's decided to put friends an' family an' a few tumble-down shacks before a heap o' cash money. Well it's too late to start shiverin' in your boots now, feller.'

Gripping the butt of his Colt, Lamb shook his head. 'I never agreed to burn down family folk,' he protested. 'An' fire's goin' to eat up every stick of timber south of Lis Etang. Where's that heap o' cash money comin' from if there's nothin' left?'

'Some o' you crackers are even dumber than you look,' Harry Grice contributed, pushing fresh cartridges into the chamber of his gun. 'All the fire's takin' out is your abandoned, stinkin' camp an' a few acres o' dry timber. So how about thinkin' on your prospects an' finishin' off these wretched troublemakers.'

Grice misjudged Lamb's frame of mind, even his next move. But Morton Pegg didn't. Standing back from the two men, the timber merchant saw Lamb's eyes flash, saw the man's hand draw his broad-bladed knife from the sheath looped around his shoulder.

Grice had already turned away. Lamb had taken half a step forward, was lunging for the kill when Pegg fired.

Grice whirled, cursing venomously as Lamb collapsed at his feet. He pointed his Colt down at the big man's body, then at Pegg. 'Right now you need me more than him, I guess,' he said. 'But thanks anyway.'

Pegg nodded. 'I won't make a habit of it, if you don't,' he replied dourly.

'One less to divvy with.' Grice looked out across the flat, empty compound. 'What's Savoy up to, I wonder,' he said. 'He might have age, but he's still as slippery as one o' them goddamn eels they're so fond of.'

'Yeah. Do you reckon our boys'll have turned for town by now?' Pegg asked him.

'Depends. It don't sound like they're out *there* anymore. An' none of 'em are givin' up on a chase. Rogan's head is where their full pay is. I got a gut feelin' it was him that Homer went after. An' where the hell's our goddamn mayor?'

'He's stayed behind for some reason. Something must be keeping him.'

'I can only guess what,' Grice decided. 'If he talks after fillin' his gut with whatever juice he's found, it's the beginnin' of the end for us.'

Harry Grice's instinct for survival kicked in. He listened for a moment, considering the options. 'I'll find him. If one of Savoy's lot hasn't got to him, *I* will,' he warned. 'You'll have to take care o' you.'

Grice ran straight from the cookshack, cursing and ducking as two bullets whined past his head. 'If they decided against huntin' ducks, I'd be a dead man,' he wheezed.

Grice was standing in the doorway of the Boudro cabin, a humourless grin on his spare features.

Inside, Jack was kneeling beside Marney's body. Instinct made him turn and look up. *I should have reloaded*, was his immediate and depressing thought. *Talk to the son-of-a-bitch*, was his second. *It doesn't matter about what.*

'Tell me, Grice,' he started. 'How's anyone going to believe that a man who manages to live with a horse turd for a brain, gets involved in a high-priced business deal? Mercenary killings, yes. But a *business* deal?'

Grice was struck with indecision. Finding Jack Rogan wasn't what he was expecting. The hired gunman should have shot, but his sudden challenge was to reply. 'I'm guessin' our unlucky mayor didn't have time to tell you much, before you shot him,' he said.

Not wanting to make eye contact with Grice, Jack looked back down at Marney's face. On the hard-packed dirt floor of the cabin were scraps of grass matting, and he grasped a piece the size of a dinner plate. In one fast, smooth movement he launched it across the room in a spinning cloud of dirty, acrid dust. He sprang sideways from his crouched position, saw Grice push one hand to his face and bring the Colt down and across towards him.

Grice fired, and Jack felt a breath-like sensation as the first bullet thumped past his left ear, crashing through the wooden shuttering behind him. He cursed, realizing he had meant to grab the gun while the man was rubbing his eyes. He took a frantic lunge forward, swerving from the weapon as Grice clawed at the debris stinging his eyeballs.

Jack changed his mind and leaped back across the room. Grice fired blindly, and one bullet ripped into the wood close to his elbow. He grabbed at and wrenched out a brace from beside the doorway. Hampered by its awkwardness, he jumped from the steps of the cabin, thrusting and dragging it across the planked landing into the damp, gleaming eel grass. He looked back long enough to see that Grice, although half blinded, was charging towards him. There was no chance of getting to his sorrel, not enough time. He could hear Grice's enraged thrashing as he followed, now less than thirty feet behind.

Jack's breath came in long rasping spasms, as he sickeningly realized how defenceless he was. Working his way through discarded eel traps, ropes and nets, he wouldn't even make it to the tree cover ahead of him.

The dense bankside reeds offered immediate cover and, still running, he plunged headlong through them and into the dark bayou water. Spitting and taking desperate breaths, he struggled for balance, ramming the post into the tall reeds for support.

Seconds later, Grice appeared on the bank, lurching, then stiffening as his eyes squinted into the darkness, sighting Jack below him.

The post was over six feet long, and thicker than a man's arm, but at the moment of impact was more responsive than a dentist's probe. A single desperate exertion released it from the cloying mud and roots, sending it uncontrollably upwards. Jack's stomach heaved when he sensed Grice's jawbone being pulverised. Wildly disturbed in the stillness of the damp air, the crunching sound reverberated madly around his head as he instinctively pulled away. Grice's skull snapped back, his body buckled forward, arching into the tall reeds directly above Jack's head.

He thrust again at the falling body, getting a foot-hold in the thick mud and trodden vegetation around his legs for the plunge into Grice's stomach. The body crumpled on the post, transforming itself into a lifeless dummy, but still menacing against the deep blue skyline. With one hand still gripping the post, Jack clawed frantically at the bank, his eyes fixed on Grice's shattered face. But as he drew himself upwards, he watched with dread as a wave of consciousness returned to Grice. He froze as an outstretched arm twisted towards him, closing his eyes as the barrel of the man's fine, blued-steel Colt pushed into the centre of his forehead.

Grice pulled the trigger as Jack's face drifted into agonizing focus. But the livid clarity spun away almost within the same instant.

At the lethal gunshot, Jack's arms and legs swept outwards in a single convulsive movement, and through the dazzling explosion he had a vision of Melba Savoy. She was a lightning portrait, her arms outstretched, as he catapulted backwards to the water beneath him.

Jack's revulsion at the water returned his senses. He was unharmed, but his body reacted instinctively as the dead weight of Grice's body crashed against him. The air was driven from his lungs and he slithered sideways, gagging as the water rushed into his nose and mouth. Then he gave a fierce kick, freeing himself for the distance to shove the body away from him.

'You should have rode on,' he gasped. 'Should have rode on the first time I beat you.' Jack suddenly imagined what other wildlife was in the water around and behind him, and he shuddered violently. He made frantic efforts to climb out, looked up and yelled. 'Help me. Get me out of this goddamn place!'

There were voices and Jack felt his hands and arms being grabbed. Then there was a hand on his shoulder and he was looking into the face of Melba Savoy.

'Thank you. You and those rabbit bones,' he said, smiling wearily.

Nearby, Sheriff Buckmaster was holding a lantern. He stood very still, watching impassively as Melba and Gaston Savoy helped Jack out of the water, easing him through broken trampled reeds and long grass onto the bank. For a long moment, the only noise was the squawking of a distressed wood duck and the rasp of deep breathing. Jack hunkered down, looked towards the sheriff and managed to find a few words to say.

'From now on, Sheriff, you better look and listen a bit more than you have been. The signs were all there to see.'

'Nothin' like this will happen again, Rogan. Not if you're not around. Right now, I've got felony reports, bodies an' prisoners to think about. It's gettin' late, so if you'll excuse me ....'

Jack looked up at the sky, blinking to return more sharpness to his vision. There was a rumbling sound he didn't at first recognize, then a crashing bellow that seemed to fill the sky like thunder. He shook water from his ears, realized it was thunder, and soon the first fat raindrops struck his upturned face. 'This *is* some other time, isn't it?' he muttered. 'Some other place.'

Two days later, after the rain, Jack was sitting with Melba and her father outside the High Chair Saloon. They had spent most of the morning explaining the affair to Beatrice Marney and Elspeth Tedder.

'What happens when someone else discovers what was goin' on ... when it all comes out?' Gaston Savoy was asking.

'You all keep quiet and it won't,' Jack said. 'Let them all assume the Department of the Interior *is* looking after the land. It's in no one's interest to let on. And that Chester feller's not going to spill the beans. Him or Bunce. Wherever they are.'

'What about those who were killed? Someone's responsible for my husband's death,' Elspeth Tedder said.

'And mine,' Beatrice Marney added.

'Prices have been paid. Some have been higher than others, but to a degree we're all in there,' Jack replied. 'I'm thinking rough justice is probably better than opening a great big can of worms. Milo Buckmaster must give an appreciative nod to that – want to keep it in the family, so to speak.'

'An' the timber?' Gaston Savoy asked. 'How do I deal with that problem?'

'If the railroad's needing ties let them log some remote corner. Be smart ... keep an eye on their movements. Share out the profits. Ask them for something in return, like a new home for those orphans – *their* orphans. How about new roads across the town? You'll be able to live a better life. Now you've got to know the town and its folk, what's there to feel inferior about? What do you say?'

Melba had been quietly watching the last of the raindrops drip from the honeysuckle. 'I'd say, it's all right for you,' she offered. 'Beaumont, Texas is many miles from here.'

'That's true,' Jack started. 'But with all those investors and their money sloshing in and around Whistler, I've been thinking maybe there's new business for me here in Blackwater. I could build myself up a pension.'

'Opportunities don't wait, as Pa would say. But what about your family?'

'When your pa gives me back my money, I'll forward

it on … all of it. I'll tell them I'm okay. That way, at least some of us make a gain.'

Melba looked to her father, who gave a slow, wise grin.

'I think the man's right. I guess it's never too late for any of us to do that,' he said.